SALT

CATRIN KEAN

SALT

Gomer

For my dad, Peter: thank you for the stories

And for Ellen and Samuel, wherever you may be

First published in 2020 by Gomer Press,
Llandysul, Ceredigion SA44 4JL

ISBN 978 1 78562 319 6

A CIP record for this title is available from the British Library.

© Catrin Kean, 2020

Catrin Kean asserts her moral right under the
Copyright, Designs and Patents Act, 1988
to be identified as author of this work.

This book is published with the financial support of
The Books Council of Wales.

Printed and bound in Wales at
Gomer Press, Llandysul, Ceredigion
www.gomer.co.uk

'*Someone, in another time, will remember us.*'

Sappho

Chapter 1

Smoke

1941

It is ice-bright, the night of the bomber's moon.

In the front room of a terraced house next to the graveyard Ellen Jordan lies in bed. Her fingers worry rosary beads and she spits curses at the devils who head over the sea towards them, intent on harming her family who huddle, blanket-wrapped, in the gaslit Anderson shelter in the back garden.

In the shelter Ellen's son Louis, an unlit cigarette between his lips, fiddles with the wireless knobs to try and find the World Service. Strange voices from across the sea fade in and out as he twiddles, thumping it with his fist every now and again as though that might help.

'Do we really want to know?' asks Mary. Her Irish voice, her Irish prayers, spoken silently as she knits with fingers swift as spiders. The small boy Sam listens, impatient, for the bombing to start. As soon as the all clear is sounded he will be out in the alleyways searching for shrapnel treasure until the sirens howl and everyone skitters for shelter again.

His sister, Ellen's blackberry-haired girl Teresa, reads *Nelson's Jolly Book for Girls* with a frown of concentration, Reggie the corgi on her lap, his legs running in a dog-dream. Louis finds the BBC news bulletin at last, holds a match to his cigarette and sits back to hear what their fate might hold.

On the other side of the city a Caribbean man, Noah Best, patrols the silent streets, his steel helmet heavy on his head, his woollen coat buttoned up to his chin. His legs are bowed, sculpted by the sea that has rolled beneath him for most of his life, and the icy air stabs his bones. He is looking for splinters of light in windows, light that will offer them all to their enemies, though the moon, big and fat as a peach, is doing that job very well.

'Turn that light out,' he shouts, seeing a faint glow behind a window. His voice echoes in the silver night. The light dies and he walks on. He is looking not only for lights but also for people who are lost, who need taking to safety, but there is no one. He is alone in the petrified streets.

The city is pewter in the moonlight, waiting, holding its frozen breath. Families huddle in home-built shelters or in cellars and tunnels under the city. He thinks of Ellen, who is not in a shelter. Tonight he is breaking a promise he made many years before, to keep her safe.

Tonight he can't help her. The bombers are coming. They fly in over the sea in a swarm, hunched and hellish. Panicked seabirds rise up out of the quiet dark and are slivered by the propellers. And on they come, and on.

And then the city explodes.

'You fucking devils,' screams Ellen as the first bomb hits. But after that she can't hear her own voice. She has seen the rage of the planet before but not like this, nothing like this.

The explosions pull pictures from walls, hands from clocks and crockery from shelves. The statue of Our Lady lies with her blush-pink face in pieces and rosary beads rend and fly. Ellen closes her eyes and sees trees ripped from the ground, mountains set alight, the dead spat from their graves.

Then, the biggest blast of all and the heavens fall in. The blackout curtain rips from the window and glass rains around her head and the midnight sky is bright as day. She hangs onto the bars of the bed, her hands blue and translucent in the awful light, as she wills herself to another place and time, rocking on a man's heartbeat.

Then there is silence, apart from a sound like a tide washing in.

'No need to make such a fuss,' a man's voice says in a Caribbean drawl. A sea-shanty voice. She opens her eyes and sees a black man standing outside the window, his hair a silver halo in the bright night. He is smoking a Woodbine, calm as anything. The smoke curled in the frozen air. It's Samuel.

'Why they leave you here on your own?' he asks.

'I'm a silly old woman,' she says. 'I tripped on the stairs and broke my hip. It's in as many pieces as those plates in the kitchen. I can't even pee by myself now.'

She remembers his handsome face. A thoughtful face, she thinks.

'You need a barber,' she says, and he laughs.

'Wanderers have no need for barbers.'

A wanderer. That was what she was, once, and in a way she still is now. They say she is losing her mind but in truth she is letting it go, a kite in the wind. She has a thought, to get up and go with him, but then she remembers her broken old body.

'You seen Bright?' she asks. Another wanderer, Bright was.

'He's been around.'

'Expect he needs a barber too.' He always needed a barber, did Bright. He could have had a whole family of birds living in his beard and nobody'd ever have known.

Fingers of iced air have slipped into the room and the sky flashes behind Samuel like God's own firework display, making a silhouette of him. She can see her own breath, but not his. Only the curling wisp of smoke from his cigarette. Reminds her of something.

'It's the end of the world,' she tells him.

He shakes his head. 'Even those bastards aren't bad enough to end the world.'

She believes him, and she is pleased. Not for herself, as she is tired and ready to go, but for the children.

'They're in the shelter,' she says. 'Louis built it. He's a good boy; you'd be proud of him.'

He nods, but he seems to be thinking of something else. He isn't looking at her any more. She looks at his face, still lovely in old age, and an ache passes through her.

'Come in out of the cold,' she says.

'I can't do that,' he says. 'You know I can't.'

She closes her eyes and she knows he has gone. Two tears slip down her cheeks, warm against her china-cold skin. She is alone again, and as sound bleeds back into the room she becomes the exploding world itself, the white-hot pain in her bones the pain of the murdered earth. She can't pray because she has no words left and she can't cry as her tears have burned away.

She waits to be turned to dust.

It is a long time later, another lifetime, that there is a siren, footsteps, voices. There is a clammy hand in hers and the scent of a child who smells sweet, of earth, of under the ground.

'You're like an angel, Granny. Covered in stars.'

'It's not stars, it's glass.' Mary, pulling Teresa away. 'Oh good god, she's frozen.'

Ellen no longer feels cold but she is aware of the trembling of her body. She feels blankets being wrapped around her, hears a coal scuttle being dragged across the floor. Further away she can hear the sirens and bells of the shocked city.

Then another voice. 'I came as soon as I could.' She recognises Noah's voice, sees his shadow in the doorway taking off his hat. He sits by her bed.

'It's over now,' he says. His lovely island voice. She was on that island once, a long time ago. She remembers the sound of

11

the wind in the tall sugar cane and the strange birdsong. And then she remembers running along a dust track, salt sweat in her eyes, running after a man whose heart had been broken.

She thinks to mention Samuel's visit last night but then decides against it. She closes her eyes as Noah rubs warmth back into her hands. The voices dance around her. Whole streets gone, they say. She can't imagine it, how a street can be there and then not. How is the world so frail?

And then Teresa's voice, anguished. 'Oh no, look.'

Teresa holds the pieces of a blue sea-washed bottle. And in the palm of her hand a small ship made of driftwood and toothpicks, broken in the storm. Ellen reaches for the ship, picks apart the pieces.

'We can fix that,' says Noah but around them Mary is sweeping, sweeping glass and small smashed treasures, sweeping it all away, and it is too late because something has gone that cannot be fixed or replaced.

The small curl of smoke from the ship's chimney.

Chapter 2

A Wish

1883

Two men walked up from the dock, canvas bags slung over their shoulders. The town was hot with a strange wind, foundry smoke and ash shimmying against a hidden sun, gulls riding on winds that moved in from faraway places. The wind shivered the mud flats, rippling the black water that gullied the town: the docks, canals, timber ponds and rivers. The men walked past the staiths and warehouses, past the boarding houses and seamen's missions, unsteady, as though the ground under their feet was not solid, and they laughed about it, feeling easy.

In the small back kitchen of a terraced house in Grange Street, Ellen hauled steaming sheets from a pot and carried them outside, hot breath rising from them. She hung them and pulled the washing line rope to let them fly. Beyond the high wall of the garden she could hear the chug and grind of the port.

A child had followed her outside, was crouching, digging in the dusty flowerbed. She yanked his arm, pulled him inside, scrubbed at his hands and knees as he wailed in protest.

'Your Mammy said you have to stay clean today.'

Flies whined and slapped against the window as she pulled fat bread out of the oven and set it to cool, swatting another child's hand away from it. She scooped the baby up from the floor and settled him on her bony hip, smelling his milk-stench, and looked out of the grime window to the white sheets twisting and clasping each other in the wind, and she wished, and she wished. Her brother Bright was expected home today, bringing gifts and stories. Bright had seen the whole world. She loved him and she also hated him because he had been born a boy and she hadn't. His world was everywhere and hers was here.

But there were plenty of others who would take this job: the scrubbing and steaming, helping Mrs Watkins keep body and soul together with her sea captain husband away. Plenty of others who would smack and starch, boil and wash and spit the tears away from the faces of children she pretended to love.

She took the children upstairs, dressed them in their starched sailor suits, lined them up like skittles. Push one and they'd all go over, she thought. She heard a man's voice in the hallway downstairs. Mrs Watkins appeared in the doorway, her face tired, though Ellen didn't know why because she never did anything. 'Ellen, you may go. My husband's ship has docked.'

If her husband's ship had docked it meant Bright's ship had too. Ellen handed over the baby and ran down the stairs. From behind the half open door of the front parlour came the sweet scent of pipe tobacco smoke. Ellen pulled open the front door, and ran.

The wind was combing the long grass on the moor. She ran, and seeds flew fairy-like round her head. She ran, and gulls dived above her. She ran – and then something caught her foot and she fell, sprawling in flattened grass, dust in her mouth, a horse's head jerking up above her with its eyes wide.

She unhooked the horse's rope from her ankle and got to her feet. She soothed the horse – hush, hush. The breath of it on her hands, warm. She brushed grass seeds off herself and then saw, in the brown fabric of her skirt, a rip where a thorn had caught it. Mammy would have to fix it, if she didn't have the devil in her today.

Mammy had brought the ghosts of the Great Hunger with her when she came from Ireland.

Ellen ran again.

Off the moor, through the maze of workers' cottages, boys playing, women scrubbing steps. In Coke Street a group of women stood in a gossip group, staring at her house.

'Is Bright home yet?' she called to them but she didn't wait for the reply. She pushed open the door ready to greet her brother, who sat smoking by the fire, barefoot, his feet fat as jellyfish. She took in his weathered sea-skin, his matted beard, his pale eyes, and he stood up and held his arms wide for her, and she put her face against his lovely chest and smelt the sweat and the sea on him, her big bear. But then she saw what was behind him, in the kitchen.

Mammy was smiling, which was a strange thing in itself. And standing beside her was a dapper African man, grinding salt between his fingers and sprinkling it into a pan of bubbling stew.

'Bright's brought his friend to visit us. Ellen, meet Samuel.'

The man turned and smiled and stepped out of the kitchen to greet her. He was about twenty-five years old, the same as Bright. His hair was cropped close to his head and he wore a beard, short and tidy. He had high cheekbones and narrow, thoughtful eyes that creased when he smiled. 'I am honoured. Your brother speaks of you a lot.'

His voice was low, and slow, and he savoured the 'r's as though he was tasting them. Ellen bobbed the way she did when she greeted her employer, and her hand went to her skirt to hide its shameful rip. She realised she must have dust on her face and her hair had come loose from its pins.

'Samuel is a cook,' said Mammy. She had become girlish and her cheeks were pink. 'So he is cooking for us tonight.'

Ellen smiled; how nice. She excused herself, and ran upstairs. She took Mammy's sewing box from a shelf and sewed up the rip, wondering why her hands were shaking.

She came downstairs and lit the lamps, pulled the curtains across, stoked the fire. Samuel ladled the stew into bowls and set them on the table and they all sat down.

'Bless us oh Lord and these thy gifts which we are about to receive from thy bounty,' said Mammy, speaking fast and tripping over her words. 'And thank you Mr Jordan.' At which he smiled, and nodded, and then they all picked up their spoons to eat.

The stew was flavoursome, far better than Ellen and Mammy had ever made. Mammy was happy, laughing, no sign of the devil in her. Bright and Samuel told stories of the sea, of men who had fallen overboard, of brightly coloured flying fish, of birds who hitched rides and stayed with them for miles. Bright watched Ellen, amused at her silence, as usually on his homecoming she couldn't stop talking. He had brought her a present, a seahorse, a tiny thing. She held it in her palm and listened as Bright described finding it on a beach in West Africa, where he and Samuel had washed their feet in seawater warm as a bath.

She decided to speak, at last. 'Which part of Africa are you from, Mr Jordan?'

Samuel laughed.

'I am not from Africa,' he said, and she felt her cheeks burn. She was so stupid. It would have been better to have stayed silent.

'My ancestors came from Africa,' he said. 'But I was born on a small island in the Caribbean sea. It is called Barbados.'

Barr-bay-dos. The name sounded lovely to her but she was too shy to ask more. She filled their mugs with beer from the jug and went to sit by the fire, and listened to the men talk, and wished again that she had been born a boy.

'Have you ever been onboard a ship?' Samuel asked her, half turning in his chair to look at her. She shook her head.

'You should take your sister,' Samuel said to Bright. His voice always sounded as though it had a smile in it.

'You don't want to be putting more nonsense in that girl's head than is already there,' said Mammy, gathering bowls. Samuel got to his feet and nodded his head to Mammy.

'Thank you for your hospitality,' he said. 'I'll be returning to the boarding house now.' He grinned at Bright. 'And let you take that bath.' Samuel had already bathed at the boarding house and the men had joked about it, how Samuel was so clean and Bright so dishevelled.

'See our guest out,' instructed Mammy, and Ellen went with Samuel to the door.

'It was very nice to meet you,' she said. She handed him his coat and hat from a peg on the wall and opened the door. He stepped outside, and started to walk away.

'Wait,' she said. He turned. She glanced over her shoulder, heard Mammy's giggly voice in the kitchen as she unhooked the tin bath from the wall to prepare for Bright.

'Would you show me?' Ellen asked. 'The ship.'

'Your mother might not like that,' he said. She didn't answer and there was a moment when neither of them spoke. But then … 'Yes,' he said. 'Of course. I will arrange it.'

She stood in the doorway watching his slight shape walk away in the darkness, and she was aware that something strange had happened to her body. It was like the centre had fallen out of her, left her drifting in the wind.

Chapter 3

Labyrinth

1883

On good days, when she didn't see dead people wandering about the place, Mammy took mending in. The African visitor who wasn't African had been good for business, as curious neighbours wanted a reason to come and ask about him. On Sunday after Mass she settled by the fire with her sewing machine and Ellen managed to slip out without her asking questions, feeling pretty in her Sunday best.

Samuel was waiting for her on the corner. He seemed different, quieter than when he had been in her house. They walked the edge of the moor, past rows of smart shipowners' houses, down towards the dockyard. She wasn't shy today. She told him about her work for Captain Watkins' wife, about the children who were naughty and about Mrs Watkins who was lazy. Samuel said nothing as she chattered, except to ask her whether she liked the work.

'Of course not!' she said, giggling at the thought of it. 'Do you like yours?'

He shrugged. 'It's a part of me,' he said. They were approaching the dockside. She had heard the docks, the song of the town, every night and day her whole life. She'd watched the ships with Bright when she was a child, sitting on the cliff looking down. But she had never been this close before. The noise was thunderous, horses and carts, trains, chains and ropes and barrels and crates being hoisted high into the sky, women with baskets on their heads and men shouting in a hundred different languages: Somali men, and Yemenis, Greeks, Chinese, Irish, Welsh. Notices plastered on walls advertised emigration passages to New York, San Francisco, Melbourne. The air was scented with salt and sweat and smoke. She was jostled, and moved closer to Samuel.

And then there was the ship. It was a gigantic iron thing, red-painted, taller than she'd ever imagined, as high as a cliff. A stream couldn't hold a skimmed stone, so how did the sea hold this? It had webs of high rigging and flags fluttering from the mast, bright and slap-slapping at the clouds. Samuel told her to wait, and went to talk to a group of men who were standing together and smoking. They glanced back at Ellen as they spoke, and nodded. Samuel came back to her and smiled.

'Welcome aboard the *Mary Alice*,' he said, and held out his arm to her. She took it, feeling his solidity, his warmth, and they walked up a wooden staircase and onto the deck. There were men slopping it down. They looked at Ellen curiously and nodded to Samuel and she felt their deference, felt that he was a man who commanded respect, who had a presence, and she smiled to herself because it felt good to be walking beside a man like that.

She'd always imagined ships to be light, moth-like, in the way they glided over the water. But this thing was enormous and heavy. She wondered again how the water could hold it, and then she realised it was because the *Mary Alice* was a live thing. She could feel her shifting, breathing, the creak and moan of her pulse.

She followed Samuel down into her depths. It was a maze: narrow gaslit passages and steep stairs leading down, down. There was a smell of damp and oil. She could hear distant muffled sounds – the shouts of men and hammering on iron, attending to the ship's injuries.

Samuel took her into the saloon and Ellen gasped, it was so lovely – marble pillars and gilded mirrors and the seats covered in crimson velvet. She sat on one, imagining herself a lady.

'You will never usually see this part,' Samuel said. 'Unless you marry a lord.'

'Stranger things have happened,' she said, laughing. She felt like a child, like she had entered wonderland. She wondered what Samuel would say if she asked him to dance. It seemed to her that here, in this other-world, you could do anything.

He showed her the first class cabins with their ceramic washbasins and the round portholes. 'However rich you are, you still sleep with the sound of the ocean in your ear,' he said. Down they went and down, past the captain's cabin and the surgeon's and the priest's, and then into the vast dark cargo hold with its curved ribs. Ellen felt as though she had entered a strange labyrinth, and always the sea breathed its rhythm around and beneath them.

They climbed down iron ladders into the heart of her – the engine room. An enormous drum took up the middle of the space, large enough for four people to lie in end to end, and connected to that were cogs and wheels, engines, spindles, iron chains, cranks.

'The engines have the power of one thousand horses,'

21

he said. They were cold and silent but she imagined the heat and throb of them when they were working, rotating hard enough to send this iron creature across the world.

'And this,' Samuel said, opening a carved wooden door, 'is mine.' She stepped into the galley, deep in the ship's belly. She thought, if the engine is her heart, then this is her soul.

Low arched iron ceilings gave it a church-like feeling. Pots, ladles and spoons hung among bunches of dried herbs. Shelves of jars and cans, chests of stoneware flagons and bottles, and enormous cast-iron ovens.

'When these are fired,' said Samuel, 'it's hotter than the tropics in here.'

A disdainful black and white tomcat eyed them from high up on a shelf.

'What's his name?'

'He hasn't yet divulged that information to me,' said Samuel, and Ellen laughed, because he was funny, and because the day was lovely. And because this wasn't the real world but somewhere else, she stood on her tiptoes and kissed Samuel, soft, on the cheek.

Chapter 4

Earth

1883

Ellen squatted in the small back garden of the house in Coke Street, working her hands deep into the stony soil. An ivy-cloaked stone wall enclosed the garden, blocking out everything but sky. From beyond the wall Clara-next-door shouted and one of the babies cried. Clara's mother produced a baby a year, filling every corner of the house with children of all sizes. A dog barked; the trains hissed and belched as they rattled in and out of the freight yard. She remembered waiting at the yard gate for Daddy to finish work. Daddy swinging her up on his shoulders. Daddy's scent of metal and oil.

When she was little the smoke and ash from the town used to creep into her lungs, leaving her hunched and frightened, her breath imprisoned. Daddy would make her stand straight and breathe, breathe, breathe. 'In out, in out,' he'd say, his voice low and hypnotic: 'Your mind is everything.'

He taught her how to use it to free her breath. But she had never found out how to free herself. It seemed that grey walls surrounded her always, both here and at Mrs Watkins' house.

A chill moved in from the sea.

She dug deeper, making a trench around the edge of

the bed. Two chickens pecked, slow-motion, pausing with a red claw held up, perfectly still. She thought of Samuel, tried to remember his face, the smile behind his eyes, the smell of his skin when she had kissed him. Pushing her fingers deeper into the earth she felt the firm shape of a potato sleeping in its dark place, and she pulled it, dropped it in a bucket. Then another, and another.

She thought of Jacob, who came courting her. Secret, bitter kisses on the street corner and slapping his hot straying hand away. Mammy put a stop to it. 'He'll give you squat ugly babies, like little trolls,' she said.

Then there was Matthew.

'He's a bloody Baptist.'

Mammy put a stop to anyone who wanted to court her daughter. For a small woman, she knew how to block a doorway.

With Samuel, she was letting him right in. But was he courting her? She wasn't sure. He visited often, but maybe to see Bright.

The potato bucket was full. She smoothed the earth and rocked back on her heels, picking at the mud under her nails. She knew that at that moment Samuel was with Bright, drinking ale in the red Railway Hotel on the dockside. She imagined them, sitting by the window with the grey water shivering outside. She felt the cold breath of the sea through the window panes, saw their heads bent close, talking earnestly. Smoke rising.

What were they talking about?

Chapter 5

Clocks

1941

'Well it's a right mess out there.'

Mary, coming in with the weekly rations, brushing fallen strands of hair from her face. The family come and go like birds to a nest, bringing with them shards of gossip about bombs, evacuees, someone cheating on the rations. But the rhythm of Ellen's day is the ticking of clocks.

Louis collects clocks. Brass clocks, wooden clocks, clocks that chime and ring, peal and jangle. He has a wooden clock in the shape of a monkey, with eyes that roll from side to side as it ticks and a tail for a pendulum; a present from his father. The grandmother clock in the back room has a blue sailing ship rocking under its face and it rings each hour in and out with a melancholic bell. It takes Louis hours to wind them all up but he likes time to be kept, and there's a story that gets told and retold about the time he was so early for a train that he was on time to board the train before.

Some of the clocks smashed on the night of the bombing but plenty remain, ticking and rattling, shuddering and shrieking, each out of time with the other, and the throb-throb of Ellen's broken hip joins in and she feels her life ticking away in the cacophony of it all.

From her bed she can hear other noises too: the coals in the fire spit and settle, and from the kitchen a whistling kettle, a wireless, low chatter. Outside, the rumble of trams. And then, running feet.

The front door bangs open. Mary shouts 'Take your shoes off,' from the kitchen. Then: 'Ask Granny if she wants a cup of tea.'

Teresa stands in the doorway and repeats stonily. Do-you-want-a-cup-of-tea. Even without seeing her Ellen knows she's been crying. 'Yes I'd love one,' she says. 'And then come sit with me. If I wasn't dying of old age I'd be dying of boredom. Nothing to listen to except those bloody clocks.'

Teresa brings tea, helps Ellen sit up, fluffs the pillows. Her eyes are puffy but Ellen knows better than to ask direct. She also knows that Teresa can't talk to Mary, who will just snap at her to pull herself together. 'Sticks and stones,' she'll say. Mary learned long ago, in her Dublin orphanage, that emotions were shameful things, things to be buried. 'Put your corns in your pockets,' the nuns would tell her when the mismatched shoes she was given hurt her feet. Now Mary puts everything that hurts in her pocket, tucked out of sight.

And Louis? Louis lives in a different world from everyone else, Ellen thinks. Almost as though he's flying high above everyone's heads. She has never quite been able to fathom this dreaming son of hers.

He is so like his father.

'Good day in school?'

'Boring.' With a shrug. Teresa wishes that the school had been smashed into a million pieces by the bombs. She is pulling at her hair. 'Granny can I cut my hair?'

'No, you cannot. What a thought. Such beautiful hair you have. You and your brother.'

Teresa makes a face. Sam's hair is blond, a gold halo around his head, and his eyes are green.

'Bring me a comb,' says Ellen. 'You've got it all knotted.'

'It wasn't me,' says Teresa. 'They pulled it.' And then shuts down again but she doesn't need to say more for Ellen to know who. Those sly-eyed white girls, waiting on street corners, spitting spite. She's seen scratches on Teresa's face before now. There's a bloody war going on, thinks Ellen: haven't people learned anything? Teresa brings the comb and Ellen teases out the knots, feeling the warmth of her girl against her in the cold bed. Teresa's hair starts to fly free, curling around her head.

'Would you like me to do you a style like the girls in Barbados?' asks Ellen.

'No!'

'So pretty they were,' says Ellen, remembering. 'So pretty with their plaits and ribbons.'

The combing and finger-teasing is hypnotic. She feels Teresa's body soften, relax, as though Ellen is pulling the spite out of her hair, piece by piece.

Then Teresa says, 'Is it true that coloured people have smaller brains than white people?'

Ellen feels a white hot stab of anger pass through her. She knows that Teresa is hinting at only a tiny part of what was said to her today, of what is said every day. She knows that they tell her she is stupid, that her lovely skin is dirty, that her grandfather was a savage and that her grandmother is a filthy whore for marrying him. Sticks and stones, she thinks, can break your bones, but she knows, oh she knows, that words can do the worst damage of all.

'Your grandfather was the cleverest man I ever met,' she says. 'He read books like you wouldn't believe. He could speak nine languages! You ask those girls, how many languages can their fathers speak. And then come back to me and tell me whose brain is smaller.'

She remembers how she stopped putting Louis, her perfect shining child, out in his pram on the front doorstep after she found spit on his face. Ellen puts her papery arms around her granddaughter. She thinks, I really want to hold my husband. I need to hold my husband. Please Samuel, she thinks. Come back.

And the salt tears fall.

Chapter 6

Coffee

1883

Ellen took the kettle from the stove and made tea, stirred in sugar, stirred in watered-down milk. She watched Bright behind a newspaper beside the fire, pipe-smoke rising. He is always a little hidden from me, she thought. She loved him, but didn't really know him. When she was ten years old he ran away to sea. Mammy howled on finding his note. No-no-no-no. Ellen held her and said 'Hush, Mammy, hush, he'll come back.'

She took him his tea.

'Thank you.' Bright supped it, glanced round at Mammy, who was hunched over her work in the window, feeding material into her sewing machine, humming a tune that was in her head but which wasn't decipherable to anyone else.

'So what do you think of Samuel?' he asked Ellen.

She felt warmth rush to her cheeks.

'He's nice.'

He looked at her, and nodded, but didn't say any more. He dipped back behind his newspaper. Mammy's voice rose, tremulous, trilling. And Ellen, invisible again, slipped out to meet Samuel, who was waiting for her on the corner of the street.

They wound their way through the market-day crowds, past stalls of shiny apples, trays of buttons, rabbits hung from hooks, crates of squawking chickens, dozing horses. The stench of fish. Usually Ellen would be here shopping for Mrs Watkins, but today was different.

Stallholders and domestics shopping for their mistresses turned to watch them as they passed, this black man and white woman walking together, and Samuel seemed not to notice but Ellen stared back, a warning in her eyes. Her blue stare, Samuel called it. At home she was getting sick of the children who came knocking to see him, asking where he was from, whether they could touch his hair, could he speak English. 'Yes, and a damned sight better than you stupid lot.' Ellen, slamming the door in their faces.

At the end of an alley Samuel pushed open a door into a small dark cafe. '*Buongiorno*,' he said, taking off his hat, Ellen one step behind him. The Italian cafe owner came out from behind the counter and shook his hand, and they spoke Italian and Ellen thought it was like a song with its rise and fall.

'I want you to meet someone special,' Samuel said. In the corner sat a black man, younger than Samuel. The man stood up, shy, nodded at Ellen, shook Samuel's hand.

'He is also from Barbados,' Samuel said. 'He is my very best friend. And, perfectly, his name is Noah Best.'

'I am very pleased to meet you,' said Noah, quiet. 'Samuel

has told me about you.' Ellen sat down. She saw a smile pass between Samuel and Noah and she felt important, someone worthy of being spoken about.

Behind the counter the coffee bubbled and spat over flame, black as treacle, filling the room with a strange aroma. The cafe owner brought them each a cup of it and a plate of *biscotti*. Ellen stirred the coffee round and round with her spoon, afraid to taste, as the two men chatted, gossiping, talking about things unknown, their accents broader now they were speaking together so that she only picked up certain things: a whale, a shipwreck, a drunkard, a death. She took a sip of the coffee. It was thick on her tongue, and bitter, and it made her feel floaty, rising up with the steam and smoke.

It gave her confidence. 'Do women come on the ships too, apart from the passengers?'

'Occasionally the captain will bring his wife,' said Samuel.

She thought of Mrs Watkins, imagined her sitting, grim and stoic on the deck, staring out at the endless grey sea, an emotionless figurehead.

Mrs Watkins doesn't deserve that, she thought.

It was on the way home that he stopped in the middle of the street.

'I wonder,' he said, 'whether you would do me the honour of marrying me.'

She stared at him. A woman with a heavy basket jostled her as she passed. A child sat on a step and screamed a snot-scream.

Samuel Jordan had asked her to marry him! She giggled, her hands over her mouth. Samuel stepped back and looked away.

'I'm sorry,' he said, and she realised she'd embarrassed him.

'Oh, no,' she said. 'Please don't be.' She moved closer to him, until she could smell the coffee on his breath.

'Yes,' she said. 'I will.'

And they looked at one another and laughed with the surprise of it.

Walking home, they kept glancing at one another and sharing secret smiles, but neither of them knew what else to say. They were both shocked, as though they had time-travelled and landed in a different part of their lives. Back at Coke Street everything seemed to be the same, Bright by the fire, Mammy with her sewing. But the world had slipped out of its orbit.

'We have something to tell you,' Ellen said, holding Samuel's hand tight. Her voice small, floating somewhere in the air with Bright's pipe-smoke. 'We are getting married.'

Bright raised his eyebrows and nodded, and Ellen realised he knew: Samuel had asked his permission.

Mammy folded up her sewing and said, 'Right then. I'll make the tea.'

Chapter 7

Mrs Jordan

1883

'Please Mammy. Come help me choose a dress.'

But Mammy was refusing to talk about the wedding at all. If she didn't acknowledge it, then it would not happen. If it didn't happen, then she wouldn't lose her daughter. She had started singing more loudly, more tunelessly, as though her voice itself could stop this thing.

So Ellen went alone, walking through fallen leaves into town, clutching a purse with one sovereign inside: some savings from her job and a present from Bright.

She had been to Howells department store many times, running errands for Mrs Watkins. But today its smooth stone facade seemed forbidden. She stood outside its grand front entrance. Horses and carriages clattered past and from somewhere across the road she could smell sweet chestnuts roasting. She fancied buying a bag and sitting by the canal watching ducks squabble in the bulrushes.

Ellen Jones, you have to go in, she told herself. She pushed open the heavy doors of Howells and shut out the clamour of the street for the hush and glitter of another world, the glow of gas lights reflecting in glass cabinets and mirrors, a thousand dainty clocks ticking and tinkling.

She walked up wide marble stairs, pushed open another door, and walked into the secret world of the wedding dress department. A scent of lavender and fabric draped the room. Rails of dresses lined the walls: dresses of velvet and silk, damask and satin; dresses with fur-draped necks, gold and silver thread woven through their fabrics; dresses decorated with jewels that glinted in the gaslight. She walked past gowns she so wanted to touch, but did not dare to.

Rising above the hush came voices from behind a velvet curtain. She walked towards them and saw, through a gap in the curtain, a languorous young woman, chestnut hair catching the light. Ellen watched, transfixed, as an assistant draped a dress over her, enfolding her secret skin in satin that changed colour, pink to lilac, as it caught the light. The fabric gushed to the floor and ran along the rug like a waterfall, while her mother moved around her, fussing and adjusting.

She would dine in the saloon, thought Ellen.

She turned to escape, but another assistant blocked her way.

'My name is Miss Roberts. May I help you?'

She was about Ellen's age, with tired blue shadows under her eyes. Ellen knew this was a hard job, had seen when shopping for Mrs Watkins how they were treated: forced to stand all day, not allowed to sit down. She saw an older assistant watching them, stern. If I leave, she'll be in trouble, she thought. Fined from her meagre wages. 'I'm getting married,' Ellen said. 'But …' She looked at the heavy, opulent dresses, feeling the weight of the single sovereign she was carrying. Miss Roberts nodded.

'Come this way.'

At the back of the room was a rail of simpler dresses. Miss Roberts took her into a marble dressing room with a vase of pink roses and a carved love seat with pink and cream striped upholstery.

Ellen watched herself in the floor length mirror as Miss Roberts undressed her to her petticoat. It was strange feeling fingers on her cold skin, brushing against her hair; it was like wind on water, making her shiver. Miss Roberts hung up Ellen's dress and slipped out through velvet curtains to fetch the first gown. Ellen looked thin, indistinct in the silvered glass. She didn't look like anyone's wife, certainly not a man as physically present as Samuel. She may as well be a fairy, she thought. Miss Roberts came in with a blue dress, slipped it over her head and laced and buttoned her into it, adjusting collar, sleeves, hem. When she'd finished she stood back and let Ellen twist and turn in front of the mirror. It buttoned up to the neck and had a bustle at the back and she immediately looked more substantial. More married.

'Blue means he'll always be faithful,' said Miss Roberts. Would he? Ellen wondered. How could she know? And how could the colour of a dress determine that? The future was a strange place now, as indistinct as the mirror she stared into.

And anyway she had seen the price: two sovereigns.

'My Sunday dress is blue,' she said. 'I'd like to try another colour.'

35

Miss Roberts came back in with a pink dress. This time Ellen looked at the tag first.

'I don't like pink,' she said, and Miss Roberts, understanding, took the dress away.

Ellen stood in her petticoat. She could hear the voices of the rich woman and her helpers, far away in this dreamlike place, and she felt alone and foolish. She took her dress off the hook. She would just have to wear her Sunday best. She was always getting above herself, thinking she was better than she was. It's just a bloody dress, she thought: no need for a fuss.

Miss Roberts came in with a cream linen dress draped over her arm, saw that Ellen was starting to get changed. Ellen saw the disappointment in her face.

'I'll try one more.'

Ellen held her arms up as Miss Roberts dropped the dress over her. It had lace at the bodice and the cuffs and an over-dress that fell open at the front like a coat. It had no bustle and fell simply from her waist to the floor. She twisted in the mirror, pinching in the material at the waist where it was a little loose.

'We can do alterations in the store.'

'There's no need. My mother is a seamstress.'

'You look beautiful, miss. Your husband is a lucky man.'

'How much is this one?'

'A sovereign, miss.'

And Ellen smiled at her reflection.

As she left, she saw the mother gazing at her daughter with a silk handkerchief fluttering around her eyes. Maybe Mammy will do the same when she sees me in my dress, she thought. Clutching the box she smiled at the young woman, who smiled back. For this brief moment, they were the same.

But when she got home Mammy wouldn't look at the dress.

The day of the wedding Mammy stayed in bed. She had refused to take in the dress, refused to speak about the wedding at all. Ellen had thought Mammy loved Samuel, not like the other boys who had tried to court her who Mammy had seen off, ferocious as a dog.

But Mammy had thought that in this case she was safe, because how could her daughter want to marry an African?

'He's not African,' said Ellen.

'Your father would never have allowed it.'

But her daddy, Llewelyn, wasn't here. He was cut in two after slipping under a coal train one dark, dreadful night. She was ten years old. The sound of the moaning trains on the track beside Coke Street appalled her now.

'Please, Mammy.' Ellen curled up against her mother's humid body. She knew her mother wanted to keep her close, was afraid to be alone in her demonic world. 'I'll do your hair and make you pretty.'

But her mother started spitting at the skeletal people who

were slinking out of the walls and Ellen could no longer reach her.

Bright, beard-trimmed and clean, walked Ellen up the aisle of St Mary's Church. Clara-next-door followed, clutching a small bunch of wild flowers. There were a few guests in the pews, all seamen in their Sunday best. Noah was Samuel's best man, nervously fingering the silver wedding ring in his pocket. The organ boomed and echoed and sweet incense rose and Ellen felt tiny in the coloured light under a weeping Jesus. Before the altar Ellen let go of her brother's arm to be married to a stranger by the name of Samuel Louis Jordan.

Afterwards they drank ale in the Birdcage Inn, and Ellen got a little giggly and held her husband's hand and kept calling herself Mrs Jordan. The surprise of it. No more Ellen Jones – someone completely new had stepped in and taken over with a lacy cream dress and a bunch of meadowsweet.

Later Samuel took her through a gaslit night to his room in the boarding house in Tiger Bay.

The room was small and dingy with a single bed and a washbasin. Her husband slipped her dress off, but she held her arms tight around herself and wouldn't let him remove her petticoat. They slipped into bed, both half dressed, and she touched his skin under his shirt, so warm, so unknown. But she was afraid. People were shouting on the stairs and in the streets and the docks were alive, working, grinding, mournful ships keening from out to sea. Pigeons muttered on the windowsill. She lay with her head on Samuel's chest, felt the rough curl of hair and his heart beating inside him. The heart of her husband: the most beautiful thing she had ever heard. And Samuel closed his arms around her and felt that he had come home.

In the morning she went home and Mammy sat up in bed and laughed and said she knew it wouldn't last. 'I'm married Mammy,' said Ellen and showed her the ring. 'I love him.' It was a strange feeling, like falling.

Mammy spat at the wall. What was love but people leaving you? Ellen got into bed and curled herself against Mammy's back and listened to her demons, and wondered where she and Samuel would live, and what would happen to them all.

Chapter 8

Flight

1883

Ellen sat in the tick-tock silence of Mrs Watkins' drawing room. Mrs Watkins sat facing her, fussily adjusting her skirts, before turning her gaze on Ellen.

'I understand you recently married.'

'Yes, ma'am.' Ellen thought to hold her hand out to show her the ring, but decided that it would not be appreciated. Mrs Watkins was rubbing her fingers. There seemed to be more.

'And I understand that he is a ...'

Tick, tock.

'A seaman,' Ellen said.

Mrs Watkins inhaled deeply.

'A Negro.'

'He is a gentleman from the West Indies, ma'am.'

Mrs Watkins nodded.

'You know, of course, that I will have to let you go.'

'Yes ma'am. I realise that being a married woman no longer befits this position.'

Ellen knew this wasn't what Mrs Watkins meant. She stared at Mrs Watkins. Say it, she thought. Say it.

But instead, Mrs Watkins stood up and smoothed her dress.

'Then I wish you all the best,' she said. Ellen stood up as well, nodded and made to leave the room. Then, to her back …

'I trust there will not be any children from this union.'

Ellen paused in the doorway. Turned.

'If there are,' she said, 'I trust they will not be brats like yours.'

She slammed the front door behind her, leaned back against it and laughed. That is what is called cooking your goose, she thought.

'Well, you'll have to get yourself another job,' said Mammy. 'He'll go back to sea again and I can't afford to keep you.'

And that was when Ellen realised that nothing had changed. She would still be here, in this small dark house with Mammy and the ghosts, and she would go to work for another Mrs Watkins, if she could find one who hadn't heard Mrs Watkins' badmouthing of her. Samuel would leave her here just as Bright had, and once a month she would stand in a queue at the Shipping Office waiting to collect her monthly allowance, and apart from that everything would be the same.

'I'm coming on the *Mary Alice* with you,' she told Samuel.

Samuel had started to wonder what he had married. Already, this shy, thin girl was starting to cause trouble.

'It's not possible.'

'You said captain's wives came onboard with them.'

'But I am not the captain. I am the cook.'

'Well what will they do without their cook?'

Samuel laughed, defeated. And so it was that he found himself sharing an ale and a smoke in the Cambrian with Captain John Stewart. Samuel had sailed with captains who were crooks, or drunks, or incompetents. John Stewart was none of these. He spoke little, but what he said was spoken with thought. His skin was sculpted from salt and wind, his hands red and knuckled, his hair the colour of sea-spray. Samuel did not know whether he had a wife, whether he would understand.

'What can your wife do?'

'She can clean, and mend.' Samuel didn't know if that was true. John was silent for a long time, sucking on his pipe.

'Is she strong?'

Samuel thought of his thin wife with her straight back, her still face, her direct gaze. Yes, he thought: I think she is.

'As an ox.'

He paused. And then, hedging his bets: 'I wouldn't like to take employment on another ship, sir.'

And John Stewart smiled a rare smile.

Chapter 9

Adrift

1883

Two days after Christmas, Mammy sat by the fire watching the coal spitting its blue flame. On the table by the window was a pile of sewing which she would soon attend to. Everything was the same. The wind still breathed in the chimney, the freight trains still moaned and rattled their way along the track at the end of the road on their way to the docks. Neighbours still stood in gossip-huddles on their front steps, though now they would have to find something else to talk about. Everything was the same, except there was one more ghost watching her from the walls.

Across town, past the freight yards and engine sheds, the smoking brick kilns and moorland, a small tug boat with a flag of black smoke raised above it pulled the *Mary Alice* out of the Bute East Dock, through the creaking iron gates of the lock, and guided her between the buoys that marked the entrance channel. Her hold was filled with coal, barrels of brandy and wine, crates of watches and cloth and ladies' clothing. On board were steerage passengers heading for a new life in America; first class passengers on an adventure; cows, chickens, pigs, a cat. There were sailors, officers, blacksmiths, butchers, stewards, winchmen, surgeons, priests, sail-makers, engineers, stokers and lamp-trimmers. And there was Ellen Jordan.

She leaned on the rail. Around her was jostle and excitement, which she tried to share, but she felt as though she wasn't there, as though she was nothing but her breath clouding in the frozen air. She watched as Cardiff became smaller, more indistinct, until the town was just a smudge, a memory, a thumbprint on glass. Then the tug set the *Mary Alice* free in the Bristol Channel, gulls diving round her sails, to join the other ships making their slow progress over the seas of the world, travelling a thousand invisible waterways.

I've done it, she thought: I've run away. Too late to go back.

Ellen used to lie in bed and imagine she could fly across the world to join Bright on his ship, sailing navy seas reflected with a thousand stars. Since Samuel had shown her round the *Mary Alice* she had added more details – the small neat cabin with the rose-painted china washbowl, the sea green and lapping out of its window. She'd imagined baking in the galley with her husband, the ship silent apart from the sound of soft winds playing round her sails. A hushed and graceful galleon gliding over the sea.

But the *Mary Alice* didn't glide. She lurched and rolled, propelled by her engines and the pulse of their invisible horses. Ellen felt the ship's heartbeat deep inside herself, in her head, in her stomach, in her bones. And there was no pretty cabin to sleep in. Samuel had hung his hammock in a corner of the galley, protecting their privacy with a curtain of sailcloth. 'Better here than in a berth in the forecastle.'

The galley, so churchlike when she had visited before, was all heat and noise. Slabs of salt fish and beef hung from the rafters along with a pig's carcass that swung, uncanny. The ovens smouldered and the pans spat, men jostled and shouted in the small space, caged chickens shrieked against their doom. The cat sat on a shelf crunching on entrails of rat.

And then:

'There's a fucking woman in the galley!'

A boy, a puny thing of no more than fourteen, was staring at her. He had wiry red hair that sprung like a fright out of his head. Ellen noted it, keeping it as an insult for later. But for now she just said, 'And there's a child in the galley!' She couldn't bring herself to use the profanity. Samuel left off from his bubbling pans and came between them, smiling at the boy.

'This is my wife, Mrs Ellen Jordan. Watch your backchat.'

The boy, whose name was Rusty, looked from Samuel to Ellen and back to Samuel with obvious surprise. He noted the warning hidden behind Samuel's smile and said nothing. But he glanced over his shoulder at Ellen as soon as Samuel had turned away and threw her a caustic look, which she returned.

She had wanted to help, to work. But while there must be a system she couldn't understand it. Noah, who was a steward, and Rusty, who was the steward's mate, came and went, bringing orders from the rest of the ship, while in the galley men shouted at one another in languages and dialects Ellen didn't know. She watched her husband, so at home in this world. It was ordinary to him. It was like watching a stranger.

There was a stench of fish and oil and men and Ellen's head hurt with the smells and the heat and the throb of the engine, and all the while the *Mary Alice* pitched beneath them. Ellen slipped behind the sailcloth to their private quarters and pulled open the lid of Samuel's tar-scented sea-chest. She took out her Sunday-best blue dress and her wedding dress and hung them from a pan hook, and put her rosary beads around her neck because in this new world you just never knew. She placed her hairbrush and soap neatly in the corner, alongside hers and Samuel's tin plates, knives and forks. Then she pulled out a cream lace tablecloth that Mammy had made, closed the chest and put the tablecloth on top.

It still didn't look like home, but something was happening inside her body that distracted her. Bile, rising into her mouth. She ran out into the main galley, her hand over her mouth, looking for a pan, a bowl, anything to be sick into.

Samuel saw her, caught hold of her arm. 'You can't be retching in here!' He led her to the galley door, past the smirking Rusty, and she stumbled up the stairs. There were people everywhere, in every passage, every corner of the ship; women with their heads in their hands, sobbing children puking into their caps. The ship stank of shit and vomit and tobacco smoke. She pushed her way through and onto the deck where she leaned over the rail and heaved into the waves, heaved everything out and then tried to breathe the air, to inhale some goodness. But the wind swept past a lady in a silver fox coat who was leaning over the rail further along the deck, across the class line, and the gust slapped her rich lady vomit into Ellen's face. More bile rose inside her and she vomited some more. She was sick until there was nothing left inside her but still her body spasmed to get rid of more.

She sat with her back against the bulwarks, her arms wrapped round herself and tried to will herself into sleep, but it was too cold, and the ship lurched too much, and she was sick again, this time where she sat because she was too weak to stand up. The sky was heavy and low with a spit of ice in the wind. The ship continued its rhythm around her; the spokes of the wheel with its slow rotations guiding the ship, the half-hourly bell tolls, the changing of the watches, the deck-scrubbing, the men in the rigging agile as monkeys, the meal-time calls, although how anyone could eat here she had no idea. Children ran, and cried, and laughed, and threw paper birds over the rail to watch them fly.

Then, as though they were one creature, the seabirds in the rigging all launched themselves into the sky at the same time and flew away, skimming the waves, going back towards the shore. The *Mary Alice* was too far out for them, in this vast grey nowhere place, and so they left Ellen alone. Adrift.

Samuel found her later, bringing with him an oilskin coat to wrap round her and a flask of port and brandy he had smuggled from the captain's supply. 'Drink this.' She sipped it. It was vile.

'It'll help,' he insisted.

It did help, a little. It made her head fuzzy and she slept a bit, the sea-wash and the sail-slap lulling her. She woke damp and stiff, and stood up. Her head was still thumping but her stomach felt steadier. She was making her way back to the galley when she heard a noise, somebody sobbing. She peered behind a pile of heavy rope coils and saw a familiar flare of red hair: Rusty crouched, his arms wrapped over his head.

'Are you all right?' she asked and he looked up, his face all snot and salt and a dribble of vomit hanging from his mouth.

'Fuck off.'

He ran the back of his hand across his face to hide the shameful evidence of tears.

She took the flask from her pocket and handed it to him. 'This'll help.'

He ignored it.

'I won't tell anyone,' she said. She remembered Bright's stories about the treatment of the new crew members, from the teasing to the tar and feathering. If anyone was to know he'd been crying ...

'I said, fuck off,' he said.

So she left him to his snot and puke.

She was sick for three days, huddled on the deck watching curtains of rain dancing towards the ship from the never-changing horizon. In the nights she lay with her back to Samuel as the hammock rocked them and the ovens ticked and spat as they cooled. He must be so disappointed in me, she thought. All my posturing, pretending to be strong.

Samuel looked at her back, turned away from him. He wanted to reach out to her but he couldn't. This was no place for her. He didn't know why he'd allowed it.

In those dark rolling nights it was as though there was a whole ocean between them.

In the early mornings she waited for him to get up first, lay there listening to him fire up the ovens, boil the coffee, stir vats of grey porridge. Then she dressed behind the sailcloth, pulling on damp clothes. Everything here, she had discovered, was damp. Saltwater seeped right through to your bones.

She was miserable but she couldn't bring herself to tell him, couldn't bear to hear it spoken, that this was all a mistake. And he knew she was miserable but couldn't bear to hear it spoken either, that it was all his fault. So there was a silence between them that felt louder than all the noise and bustle of the ship.

On the morning of the fourth day, she woke as Samuel slipped out of the hammock. She felt as though her head was made of air but she no longer felt sick. She watched as he lit the gas lamps and then pulled off his nightshirt, stood naked to the waist and washed from a pan of cold water, his back to her. The gas lights swung and painted light and shadow on him, onto the curve of his shoulders, the groove of his spine, his veined arms. He cupped water in his hands and ran them over his hair and paused with them there, long fingers resting on the back of his head. A human is a beautiful thing, she thought, especially in those quiet moments when they think no one is watching.

'I think I can eat today,' she said, and he turned to her and she could see he was glad. He brought her coffee, porridge, seaman's biscuits with guava jelly. It tasted good, salty and sweet.

The ship's compass needle swayed in its glass case, an assured and steadfast thing, guiding the *Mary Alice* towards the coast of South America. It was the last day of the year.

Chapter 10

A New Year

1883–84

Standing with her feet apart to steady herself, she stabbed a knife into a slab of chocolate, splitting it. She dropped shards of chocolate into a pan and watched it seep and glisten.

'Now add the butter.' Samuel stood behind her. She dropped a brick of yellow butter into the pan where it slid into the chocolate. She dipped her finger in and slipped buttery chocolate into his mouth. He sucked at her finger.

She liked how his eyes creased when he smiled.

She whisked eggs into mounds of silver sugar, stirred boiled plums in bubbling brandy, strained pans of boiling calves feet to make jellies, mixing in lemon rind, sherry, cinnamon, turmeric, cochineal. Next to her, Samuel cleaved the petrified carcass of the pig into belly and loin and shank. Rusty and Noah mashed mountains of potatoes, sliced beetroots, carrots, celery, and onions until tears streamed down their faces.

They were preparing a feast.

'It's curdled,' Rusty hissed in her ear when no one was watching, making her jump.

'You must have looked at it,' she retorted. Idiot boy.

She tied string around pudding bowls and put them on to steam. Samuel took the parts of the pig that were not fit for the first class table – the trotters, the head, the entrails – and placed them in bubbling vats, along with some stolen slivers of fat.

'You want me to fetch you some leather?' asked Noah, peering into the pan. This was the joke, that anything went into this broth, even the heels of old boots.

'I don't need me no leather.' A friendly elbow in Noah's ribs. Dried peas, doughballs, herbs, salt, pepper, molasses and rum were what Samuel was putting in here, before placing the vat into the enormous oven for eight bells.

Samuel prided himself on his food.

The decks were hung with lanterns that reflected, splintering, into the black water down below. Ellen had put on her wedding dress, which made her feel festive even though it was hidden under Samuel's over-sized oilskin coat and a shawl. Just before midnight Captain Stewart arrived to give a short speech, where he thanked his crew and wished the passengers a happy voyage. Then Old Joe, a toothless and milky-eyed sailor with bowed legs and skin like hessian rang out the old year, and Rusty, as the youngest crew member, rang the new one in. He was already wobbly with ale.

'Are you sure you're old enough to be drinking that,' said Ellen, as Rusty brushed past her to fill his tankard again. And Rusty, checking that Samuel was nowhere in ear-shot, retorted, 'Maybe you should go do some cleaning or something. *Girl.*'

As the *Mary Alice* pushed forward through the quiet dark under a sky iced with stars, there was singing on the decks. When the Welsh boys sang 'Myfanwy' Ellen's throat constricted, but then the Irish took over with their hand-carved fiddles and whistles, the skirl of a bagpipe: a frenzied music. Warmed from hot ale, Samuel took Ellen's arm and spun her round. She was drunk on the ale and the sweet sea air and dizzy with him, her husband. In the pauses between the tunes the sounds of a violin quartet swam in from the first class saloon, only to be drowned in another tune, faster, more discordant. More ale appeared, as well as poteen and rum, which had been hidden away in the berths to be brought out for this night. Glaze-eyed men drummed their hands on the rails, couples tucked themselves away in corners for indiscreet gropings. Someone had a fight, a spitting of blood and teeth. Samuel held her as they danced and she wanted to crawl under his skin. But then he broke away. He had seen Rusty sleeping, curled in a coil of rope like a kitten.

'He'll catch his death.'

'Let him,' she said. Samuel looked at her, a slight admonishing shake of his head, a half-smile. Then he hoisted Rusty up and took him back to his berth to sleep it off.

My husband is a kind man, she thought. A good man.

It was still black, but morning when the music started to die, the last solitary whistles keening into the blackness, the instruments spent and the players drunk. Ellen's breath clouded with Samuel's and pale rime softened the rocking silhouette of the ship. Samuel took her hand and led her through the narrow passageways, stepping over sleeping men and whispering couples. He pushed open the door to the galley.

53

The heart of the ship pumped around them and this time, in the slumbering night, she at last let him undress her behind the sailcloth, and touch her, and touch her, and oh, she sang, and oh.

Chapter 11

Downtime

1884

They slept among the glow and tap of the ovens, the hammock rolling them into one, stomach to back and legs tangled, the sound of the sea above, below and around them and the cries of nightmares and dreams calling from the steerage berths.

They woke early, before light had crept into the galley.

'What shall we do today, husband?'

'I don't know, wife. What shall we do?'

'We could go to the races.'

'Or the circus.'

'Let's go to the seaside!'

'I believe we're already there.'

This was the joke, every morning before Samuel rose to stoke the ovens, heat the water, knead the dough, before the ship woke and the kitchen became bustling again. Every morning, the two of them, curled in their rocking sea-bed, whispering, giggling. What shall we do today? As if there was a choice.

She teased his hair in her fingers.

'You need a haircut, Samuel Jordan.'

'Are you ordering me to visit the barber?'

'I'm ordering it, husband.'

She loved using the word 'husband'. It felt new, exotic, like she was a child playing being grown-up. Everything here was like make-believe.

The funny thing was, to her surprise, there actually was a barber on board.

If you put strangers together in an enclosed space, before long a town will emerge. On board the *Mary Alice* choirs were formed, sewing clubs, music lessons, Sunday schools, a weekly newspaper. Ellen wondered how the ship had ever seemed enormous to her. Now familiar, it had shrunk to a manageable size. She wandered its corridors and decks, mingling with sinewy sailors she began to know by name. Every day she talked to the pigs and to the black and white cow with her mournful eyes and hot sweet breath, all of them sad in their little pens on deck, and she let the chickens out to stretch their legs. She befriended Old Joe, the sailor who had rung out the old year. She sat beside him as he made ships out of matchsticks and splinters of driftwood and fitted them into bottles, his knuckled fingers surprisingly deft. The sea winds had etched maps into his face and his legs were so bowed you could roll a fairground ball between them. He couldn't remember how old he was but he had hundreds of years' worth of stories to tell, about seabirds and pirates, monsters and wrecks and haunted ships. 'Some ships,' he told her, 'are bad, very bad. But this is a good ship. Angels ride her rigging. If you are lucky you might see them.'

When she told Samuel he laughed. 'That Old Joe is a nincompoop,' he said.

When Samuel wasn't quiet and dreaming he laughed a lot. She liked to watch him, playing cards, or dominoes, or talking with Noah, a wet-butt cigarette between his lips. When the two of them were together they talked in dialect, a beautiful rolling sound that she could barely catch a word of. Samuel, his head thrown back, laughing at the sky.

She worked with him in the galley, kneading bread, peeling onions and potatoes, while the cat stalked the dark places for rats. Meals were at seven in the morning, at midday and at five-thirty but between that, before the preparation and after the clearing, it was their time to walk, to talk, to read. In Samuel's sea-chest were books, their pages yellow and curled with brine. If the weather wasn't too cold they'd find a sheltered spot on deck, him with a book, Ellen with the wool she'd traded tea for from a passenger. She was knitting shawls of many colours. Being associated with the kitchen, she'd discovered, had many benefits.

Sometimes Noah sat with them, smoking, watching the sea. They sat with the song of the wind and the water all around them, and the sound of the ship, the engine's heartbeat and the clapping of the sails, the quick feet of children, a burst of raised voices.

Samuel loved books in other languages. This one was Spanish: *Sab*, by Gertrudis Gómez de Avellaneda y Arteaga. She liked him to read her the words. It was beautiful, and even more so as it had no meaning for her, like whale song.

'What's it about?'

'It's about a slave who falls in love with the daughter of his owner.'

'Does she love him back?'

'No.'

When the Atlantic squalls moved in with their sideways winds and walls of navy sea, they sat supping bitter coffee on a wooden bench in the passage outside the galley. From the galley they could hear the crackle of the ovens and further along the passage, from the steerage berths, came the sounds of voices: laughter, a quarrel, a baby crying.

'Tell me about Barbados.'

He thought for a long while.

'It's a jewel,' he said at last, 'set between two seas, one sweet, one ferocious. Both of the seas are all the colours of blue and green, and sometimes purple too when a storm is arriving.'

He paused again, searching for things to tell her. 'There is a tree that they use to make maracas …'

He snapped his fingers together to show her.

'And when the wind blows through it, it plays music. We call it woman's tongue.'

He smiled.

'And there are trees that look like old, old men, with long beards. And tiny frogs sing all night.'

'It sounds lovely,' she said, but this time he didn't smile, so she didn't ask more.

Other times, curled in the hammock and awake with the wind's moaning, they talked about what the future might be like.

'Will you always be on the ships?'

'I don't know. I always fancied me a little farm. A couple of goats, a vegetable patch. Cooking me some food for passers-by maybe.'

'A cat,' she said.

'Oh yes, you have to have a cat to keep away the vermin. And I'll fetch my mother to live with us. She can help you with the children.'

She felt a shiver inside of her. There was something she hadn't told him yet: she wasn't going to have any children.

'What's your mother's name?' It was not the time to tell him now.

'My mother is Joanna.'

It was only now, on the ship, that they were getting to know one another.

She knew his father's name was James, because it was on her wedding certificate, but he had told her James was long gone. Maybe gone on the ships too, he said. He didn't know.

'Joanna.' A pretty name. Does he look like her, Ellen wondered. Did he get his dreaming face from her? They both loved the same man, she and this woman who lived on the other side of the world. Ellen imagined her, sitting in the shade of the tree that sings, staring into the beautiful face of her child.

'Does she work?'

'She works in the fields. She cuts sugar cane.'

Joanna in the sunshine, bending and snapping the cane and laying it in a basket, like bunches of sweet green flowers.

'Does she know about me?' Ellen asked.

'Of course. I wrote to tell her. Her reply will be waiting for me in San Francisco.'

Ellen imagined sitting at a table under the shade of an old-man's-beard tree with Joanna. Maybe they would be shelling peas. Joanna would be calm and gentle and not at all like her own mother. I hope I meet her one day, she thought. And I hope she won't mind that I won't be giving her any babies.

Her future stretched before her, clear as water: it would be just her and Samuel, travelling all the seas of the world together.

Chapter 12

Mary

1941

Pain runs through families like seams of salt through rock. She knows that now. When Louis was little his father's horrors would wake him from sleep, shouting in terror, and in her own dreams she meets Mammy's demons, passed down in bitter breast milk. She sees Mary's pain in her closed face, hears it in her whispered prayers, and one day Mary's children will know it too.

The house smells of cabbage heads and potato peelings. Ellen can hear Mary in the kitchen boiling a pan of kitchen waste to feed pigs who will stop the country from starving.

Mary leaves the pig broth to brew and brings tea, sits by the fire warming her palms with the cup. She is tired from the nights of bombing, from the fear.

'Louis says the Nazis have overrun Italy,' she says.

'On the ships they call tea "water bewitched",' says Ellen. She doesn't want to talk about the war.

'Oh, it sounds like a very strange life on those ships,' says Mary, thinking of something else entirely. So that when Ellen asks her whether she had ever been tempted to go to sea, she looks blank for a moment.

'Oh no,' she says. 'The mail train to Dublin is enough for me.' Every year, until the war broke out, that crowded boat, a child squirming on her lap, her head in her hands to try and stem the nausea.

Ellen has never been able to reach her daughter-in-law. Louis met her when he was in the army in Dublin. She was a seamstress at St Mary's hospital and was sitting in the sunshine in Phoenix Park, a pretty pale-eyed girl with a shy smile. Over time she has smiled less and less and now her face is shut tight as a drawer. It isn't the now that she is keeping inside, because even with the war surely she has a happy life, with her dreamy-smile husband and her pretty children. She knows she is one of the lucky ones, that she is not just a name on a long list on a stone in a lonely graveyard. But the old times won't go away, the old times with the nuns who told her she was wicked and her prayers that would never be answered. The one good thing about that orphanage, Mary told Ellen once, was that she was taught to play the piano. There was a piano here, and Louis taught himself to play it. He played so well that before the war he'd play jazz piano in the clubs in Tiger Bay. Mary decided the piano, like so many other things, was her husband's domain and she never played again, except sometimes sitting on the stool with him playing 'Chopsticks' at Christmas.

'The very thought,' says Mary, still thinking about the mail train. She pauses from curling pieces of newspaper that will be used to relight the fire when it burns too low. 'I don't know how you did it.'

'When you were small,' says Ellen, 'what did you dream of?'

Because she dreamed of ships and strange lands. Of sailing away.

'Dream?' says Mary, as though she has never heard the word, and Ellen thinks she will shut down again.

But then Mary says, 'I think I dreamed of a garden.'

At the back of the house is a small lean-to that Mary has filled with a jungle of ferns. She spends hours in there, watering and tending to them, and sometimes Ellen hears her talking to them. Apart from the tiny potato patch out the back it is as close as she will get to a garden.

Ellen is glad Mary had a dream.

Mary smiles then. 'Water bewitched,' she says. 'What a thing.'

Chapter 13

Wreck

1884

One time he asked her, 'Your mother. What is wrong with her?'

'There was a famine in Ireland.'

He nodded. He knew. He knew everything.

'She was a baby but she still remembers. So she has ghosts in her head. Her sisters, her brothers, her mother. So many people lost.'

He nodded again. She didn't know then how much he understood that ghosts can live in your head, and how once they are there they cannot be expelled.

'Have you been to Ireland?' he asked and she laughed.

'Of course not. I haven't been anywhere. Have you?'

'Dublin.'

'What's it like?'

'It's a city of poets and of rain,' he said, and she smiled.

They were sitting against the bulwarks watching the sea. Ellen imagined the sea was female and was alive, a voluminous creature, a protean thing. Sometimes she was calm, silky as ribbons; sometimes full of fury, smashing herself into pieces. She was beautiful. But in her soul, she was savage, and she held terrible secrets.

Ellen was scrubbing pans in the galley when from somewhere she heard shouting; a different tone from the usual day-to-day noise. Noah came into the galley and said one word:

'Wreck.'

Samuel started a big pan of coffee: this meant there would be a lot of people out. Ellen wrapped a knitted shawl around her head, pulled on a coat and followed Noah up to the deck.

A lifeboat was being lowered down into the sea. Passengers jostled at the rails to take a look. The sea was shivering and veined and spat sharp slivers of spray at the onlookers. Ten men in the boat, tiny in the vast sea, started heaving their oars, pushing the boat against the walls of water.

When the waves dropped they revealed the soft, distant shape of a coastline, black rocks. The boat disappeared and appeared again, climbing the height of the wave and dropping down the other side, the watching passengers holding their breath until it appeared again. Ellen didn't know how it wasn't swallowed.

And then, in watching the slow journey of the boat, she saw it, the wreck, flaying on its side, its sails ripped and trailing in the water. A faint whisper of smoke snaked into the air like a plea for help. It was as flimsy as one of Old Joe's toy ships.

They waited.

What did she expect? That after a while the lifeboat would come back with grateful, shivering passengers? Even with just one child curled in a coxswain's arms. Or at the very least a half-drowned cat.

But ten men went out, and only ten men came back.

On the horizon the wrecked ship lay quiet in the waves, its horror gone, sleeping, hidden beneath the waves.

Women threw paper flowers into the sea. Rusty passed around tin mugs of bitter coffee. There was a sombre mood on board. Because now they were nearing Cape Horn.

Chapter 14

Storm

1884

The wind wailed without taking breath, and the water sang as it sloshed in and out of the scuppers. In the berths and cabins people prayed and vomited. Ellen sat in the galley and knitted.

'Take these to the helmsmen.' Noah, with trays of tin mugs and steaming coffee.

'What, now?'

Ellen looked up from her knitting to see Rusty warming his thin blue hands over one of the ovens, the only substantial thing about him his cloud of hair.

'They doing their job. Now you do yours,' said Noah. Ellen slung on a coat.

'I'll do it.'

She picked up the coffee.

'Your husband says you've got to stay down here,' said Noah.

But Samuel had gone to arrange the slaughter of the cow:

beef broth was needed for settling stomachs in these rough seas. There was no one to stop her. She threw Rusty a smirk and left.

She steadied herself against the walls as the ship lurched, trying to keep the coffee in the mugs. Little rivulets of water danced down the stairs and spray spat in, stinging her cheeks. Captain Stewart was on deck, solemn in his long coat, ghostly in the white rage. She walked, unsteady through the waves, through inches of sea flooding and retreating across the rocking deck. The wind burned her ears and snatched the breath from her mouth. The chickens squawked in fright as they were flung around their pen.

'Thanks, lass.' The helmsmen took the coffee with swollen red-knuckled fingers. The great wheel turned and the compass needle spun inside its glass case like a ouija board, as the *Mary Alice* rose up into green mountains of sea, veined as rock.

'I went out in the storm,' she told Samuel later, and he laughed.

'This is no storm. But there will be one.'

Chapter 15

Angels

1884

There were voices screaming in the wind, like demons spinning around the ship.

It was around midnight when the galley door smashed open and water crashed in, sending Ellen and Samuel toppling from the hammock and knocking the breath out of them. As Ellen struggled to her feet the water tore her wedding dress from its hook and retreated. The drowning dress, its arms outstretched, was sucked through the door and gone forever.

There was shouting from the deck and screaming from the berths. The ship pitched onto her side. Barrels rolled across the floor and pans flew from hooks. The *Mary Alice* righted herself and carried on, a stoic thing.

This was the storm.

Nobody slept that night. While Samuel and Ellen tied up the barrels, a carpenter repaired the heavy galley door, steadying himself against the frame as more water washed in and retreated. The doctor was busy in the steerage berths, splinting limbs and bandaging wounds. Morning came with just a slight lightening of the sky, which was wild with cloud and rain.

She knew Samuel would not let her, but she wanted to see the storm. If she was going to die, she wanted to face her killer.

The galley was busy, huge vats of broth bubbling and water boiling to clean wounds. Samuel didn't see her slip out. She went to the engine room, steadying herself against the walls with her hands, and found a thick coil of rope. She looped it around her neck and climbed the narrow, soaked stairs on all fours. In the doorway to the deck she waited for the last squall to die, and before another one moved in she stepped out into the tempest. Then, moving quickly, she tied herself to the bulwarks.

She had been onboard long enough to know how to tie a knot.

She could never have imagined it, this force, the rage of it. The great solid ship pitched, flimsy as paper under the mountains of waves. White water glutted through the rigging, obscuring the faint silhouettes of tiny men who worked, bowed, further along the deck. The charcoal sky was mottled with restless lights that fidgeted and flashed behind the cloud, and fingers of lightning jabbed at the mast. She might have been shouting, or screaming, or singing, but she didn't know because she could hear nothing but the voice of the storm. The wind stole her breath and blew right through her and bitter water slammed into her mouth, her eyes, her ears, washing her clean. She felt she had returned home: the sea is where we come from, she thought.

It is who we are.

Sometime later, she didn't know how long as time had become meaningless, she heard the deck door slam and Samuel stood over her, rain in his eyelashes, rivers of it running down his skin. His mouth was moving but she couldn't hear his words. He bent over her, his fingers working fast to untie her, and it was then, behind him, that she saw them, just for a second: angels, wild-eyed, riding the rigging with stars in their wings.

She started to laugh. Samuel shouted into her ear.

'It's not funny. You could have died.'

She pointed to the rigging, and he turned, and there was an enormous crack that sounded like the sky had ripped open, and a flash of fire split the mast. Men flitted for cover as it toppled down onto the deck, hitting the rail, sparks exploding as water and fire met. Then a wall of wave slammed over the deck and punched into them. And as it retreated it left something at their feet. An animal she thought, until she saw the hair – wet as seaweed, red as blood.

Chapter 16

Ice and Fire

1884

Years later she wondered what she had seen. Was it just the lightning, as Samuel told her it was, or had she seen Old Joe's angels? Whatever it was she knew, beyond doubt, that spirits roamed the seas.

The calm after a storm is a strange thing. The *Mary Alice* glided between icebergs high as cathedrals, on a sea that was silent and smooth as glass. She had been fitted with a makeshift jury-rig and her ripped sails had been mended. But the sailmaker had another job too. As soon as they had moved through the storm, before the rats could get to it, Rusty's body was stitched into his hammock and weighed down with lead shot.

The Captain read from a prayer book, little frozen clouds puffing out in front of his face as he spoke. 'Unto Almighty God we commend the soul of our brother departed, and we commit his body to the deep ...'

The ice cracked and shifted and breathed soft air across the deck, across the bowed heads, into the faces of quietly weeping women.

'… the sea shall give up her dead; and the corruptible bodies of those who sleep in Him shall be changed …'

The ice wasn't white, as Ellen had imagined. It was blue, and green and purple, with enormous caves gouged into its sides, like portals to a frozen heaven. The smaller bergs fidgeted like the worrying of horses. Ellen looked up at the rigging, wishing she could see the angels again, come to bid Rusty farewell. There were none, but there were rainbows in the clouds.

Samuel had diamonds of frozen water droplets in his hair.

A small murmur of 'Amen' rippled around the deck. The ropes under the shroud were untied and it was let go, and the splash of it hitting the water made Ellen gasp, the horror of it, this boy dropping to the bottom of a lonely sea. She thought of his mother, hanging washing on a line outside her Welsh valley cottage on the other side of the world, waiting every day for news of her adventuring son. She thought of Bright, how lucky she was that he had kept coming back to her.

And then she thought of Rusty and how unkind she had been to him. He was just a boy, the age Bright had been when he went to sea, and his posturing was all bravado. 'I'm sorry,' she said, quiet, to herself. She hoped his burial had been successful, that he wouldn't return to haunt the ship. After listening to the night-time chatter of Old Joe, she knew that sometimes they did.

The days were short and the nights were so black that if you held your hand out in front of your face you couldn't see it. The only light came from the rocking ship's lights. The wind played the rigging like a strange harp. Captain Stewart seemed never to sleep, never to go off duty after a four-hour shift as his crew did. Because now he had to navigate his ship through narrow channels, sometimes so narrow Ellen felt she could almost reach out and touch the scrubby trees that grew on sheer mountainsides that dropped straight down into the water. Fog draped the mountain-tops and snowflakes the size of half-crowns danced across the decks. They passed wrecks stranded on the rocks, rusting and abandoned, but the lifeboat wasn't launched for these ruins and no one threw paper flowers into the sea. People had been saved from them or had not, and these ships were as much a part of the ghostly landscape as the languorous sea lions who basked on the rocks and roared at the passing ship, or the skeletons of burned trees silhouetted against the sky, left over from some long-ago forest fire.

A dolphin, flipping and panicked, got caught in one of the lifeboats. Other dolphins circled the ship, calling to it, and Ellen turned her face away as a coxswain slipped down the side of the ship to slit its throat. The gleaming carcass was hauled up the side of the ship and dragged to the galley for its dark red meat to be sliced and fried. There was excitement on board at the prospect of fresh meat, and as the meal was eaten the pod of dolphins followed the ship, screaming their grief into the night.

Ellen was sitting on deck with Samuel listening to the eery night-time noises when another appalling sound came from the steerage berths. A woman, howling.

'It's just a woman birthing a baby,' said Samuel. He had heard this many times.

The woman's terrible voice carried over the rumble of the engine, over the wind, reaching into the night to the very tops of the mountains. Sleep-deprived sailors grumbled and turned in their hammocks and women rushed back and fore with boiled water and towels. Ellen pressed her fingers into her stomach, which was tight with dread.

It was some hours later, when the cursing and shrieking of the woman had finally stopped and Ellen thought that she must have died, that news spread around the ship: a baby had been born, a little girl. As the morning sky burst into fire around them, a woman brought the baby, who had been named Faith, onto the deck where she was passed round by cooing men.

'She's a beauty,' said Samuel, jiggling her. Ellen looked at the little purple face blinking crossly at Samuel, and thought she looked like any other baby, and that 'beautiful' was not a word she would have used. But she gave Faith's mother a shawl as a gift.

Old Joe took the little creature and held her up to the sky, grinning, his mouth as toothless as hers. 'No ghosts will come haunt this ship now,' he said. 'That boy can rest in peace.'

Ellen slept turned away from Samuel for a few days after the baby's birth. He thought they had quarrelled but he didn't know what about and she couldn't tell him, why she couldn't be touched, why she couldn't have that happen to her.

On the third night she gave in, and let him come to her, and she remembered Daddy saying, your mind is everything, and as Samuel made love to her she silently chanted, there won't be a child. There won't be.

Chapter 17

Punta Arenas

1884

After weeks of sea and sky and wind and rock, the distant glowing lights of a town were a welcome sight. The *Mary Alice* docked at Punta Arenas for her mast to be repaired, and Samuel and Ellen disembarked.

'I have a surprise for you,' he said.

As they walked away from the dock she gripped his arm tight, not only because the wind was buffeting in both from the sea and from the dark mountains beyond the town, but because the ground was lurching under her feet, as though they still walked on the sea.

Warm lights and chatter in a language she didn't know spilled out of the bars on the dockside, and smelled of salt and ice, of wood smoke and of something unknown and sweet.

I'm on the other side of the world, she thought.

They walked through streets of small wooden-slatted and corrugated iron painted houses, hunched together against the wind that slammed and rattled at their walls. Shadow dogs barked from alleyways. Samuel knocked on a door.

A small woman with narrow smile-creased eyes opened the door and held her arms out when she saw Samuel and hugged him.

'This is Ernestina,' Samuel said to Ellen. Then to Ernestina: 'Ellen. *Mi esposa*.'

Ernestina clapped her hands over her mouth in delight, then ushered them in to a small candlelit room where three children sat at a table, brown-skinned and pink-cheeked. They got up when they saw their visitors, excited and giggling. One of them wrapped his arms around Samuel's legs and he bent to ruffle the child's hair. There was a lot of chatter, everyone talking at once, and it seemed some of it was about Ellen because Ernestina turned and smiled in her direction.

The room smelled of smoke and wool. A large wooden cross hung on the slatted walls beside a framed picture of Our Lady, blue-skinned and weeping. Ernestina went to a stove where a copper kettle steamed, and poured hot water into a gourd, chatting over her shoulder to Samuel in a sweet, high, sing-song voice. The children were sitting back at the table now and staring at Ellen curiously.

Ernestina sat down and drank from the gourd with a straw, before passing at to Samuel, who drank and passed it to Ellen.

'Don't say thank you unless you don't want any more.'

Ellen sucked at the straw. Ernestina smiled at her, while saying something to Samuel.

'She asks if you like it.'

Ellen nodded, though she wasn't sure. It was a little like tea, but with a taste like a bitter herb. Samuel told her to pass it on, and she gave it to the child next to her. They sat like this for some time, Ernestina refilling the gourd and passing it round, Samuel and Ernestina chatting. Ellen tried to catch words but she was tired and they were as ephemeral as the smoke and steam that drifted under the ceiling. Sometimes Samuel translated.

'Her husband is away working as a shepherd.'

'The smallest child has been ill with a cough.'

Then he stood up. 'I leave you now. Ernestina will look after you. I come and get you tomorrow.'

Her eyes widened.

'Your surprise is a night in a proper bed, better than anything those first class ladies will find,' he told her, pleased with himself.

'On my own?'

'I have things to sort out in the galley. The drinking water has salt in it.'

Ellen sat on a small bed in a candlelit wood-panelled room with a small jar of purple lupins on the windowsill, while Ernestina filled a tin bath with buckets of steaming hot water, chatting and smiling as she worked. Ellen nodded and smiled as though she understood. The wind beat a metallic, melancholic rhythm against the house. When Ernestina had finished Ellen said the word Samuel had taught her.

'*Gracias.*'

'*De nada,*' said Ernestina, and left.

Ellen sat in the bath soaping her hair and her body, pulling knots out of her hair with her fingers. Her body felt different after all this time on the ship, her legs and her stomach muscled, taut. An enormous moon spilled light through the window, onto the flowers, across the floor. She remembered when she was a small girl Mammy chanting to her: 'The man in the moon came tumbling down and asked his way to Norwich. He went by the south and burnt his mouth by supping cold pease porridge.' And Ellen giggling because it was true, there was a man in the moon. She could see his face watching her on cold winter nights.

But here the moon had no face.

When the water had turned cold and grey she dried herself quickly, as the room was chilly, blew the candles out and got into the little bed. Through the window she could see mountains, moonlit and snow-topped and strange. Then from deep in the wilderness, a puma called, her voice echoing across the night. Ellen pulled the blankets close around her.

Just before she fell asleep she wondered, how does Samuel know Ernestina?

Chapter 18

Valparaiso

1884

A pod of whales leapt out of the ocean, waterfalls streaming off their tails as they soared into the light.

They disembarked in Valparaiso. In the harbour the ships lined up in the blue water, neat and patient as horses, and bright painted houses rose up steep from the shore. Ellen bought a postcard with a picture of a horse and cart on to send to Mammy.

They wandered the bustle of the market. Ellen stopped at a stall selling silky alpaca wool in all the colours of the earth, of fruit and of berries. Samuel spoke in Spanish to the stall holder who wore her gleaming black hair in two plaits, thick as rope.

'It's good wool,' Samuel told Ellen. 'It keeps out the damp.'

'Then I'll make you a gansey with it.'

Ellen picked out a ball of berry-red wool, smelt its animal scent, held it against Samuel's face. She turned to the smiling stallholder.

'He looks handsome in this colour? *Si*?'

The woman laughed and nodded. *Si*. There was a short barter with Samuel and then he handed her some money.

'*Gracias.*'

They wandered on, Ellen with her arm linked through Samuel's. She bought some cloth to make herself a dress to replace the wedding dress the sea had stolen. But it was fruit and vegetables that they were here for. For the next few days the passengers and crew would be treated to a feast. For now, no more sea pie, lobscouse, dried pork or soup and bouilli. Samuel's hand hovered over baskets and baskets of bright coloured fruit, the like of which Ellen had never seen before: apricots, figs, pomegranate, peaches, cherries, grapes. And vegetables with enormous wrinkled green leaves, or weird and twisted like some votive offering, or purple and plump. There were baskets of chillies and peppers, red, green, yellow. Samuel pressed flesh, inhaled the scents. He showed her how to say their names:

'Cher-i-moy-a.'

'Pap-ay-a.'

He filled a donkey cart with sweet smelling fruits and strange vegetables. Then a boy led the donkey back to the harbour for loading and Ellen and Samuel followed, Samuel happy because he was going to be doing what he loved best in the world: to cook.

As Samuel sorted out the galley, Ellen sat in the shade on deck and wrote to Mammy.

Dear Mammy, I am in Valparaiso in Chile. It is hot and pretty with painted houses of different colours. The last place we docked at was Punta Arenas, which is also in Chile but very different, cold with a wind blowing in from the mountains. In the sea close to that place there are icebergs that look like huge blue cities.

This is a hard life in many ways but I hope I can keep on sailing the world: it has so many beautiful secrets I want it to show me. Our next stop is San Francisco and after that, who knows. I dream of visiting everywhere.

I hope you are well.

Your loving daughter, Ellen.

Chapter 19

San Francisco

1884

A huge dragon snaked through the streets, its writhing body all the colours of the rainbow, its mouth wide in a terrible smile, turning its head from side to side to stare at the crowds with its motor car headlight eyes. Firecrackers spat all round it. The balconies of the wooden houses were decked in paper flowers and bright banners with beautiful writing on that Ellen couldn't read, that Samuel couldn't read even though he spoke a little Mandarin. Women fanned their cinnebar-painted faces, dressed in ornate silk dresses. The air carried the scents of delicious food.

Ellen gripped onto Samuel's arm and stood in a jostling crowd, amazed. They were in San Francisco, the gold rush city. The city of dreams.

They had docked 153 days after they left Cardiff. As the ship's Welsh cargo was unloaded Ellen and Samuel went to look for somewhere to stay. They found themselves a small, airy room at the top of a tall wooden house on a hill, where they could see the expanse of golden dunes that stretched beyond the city into forever. The air smelt of metal and meat and burning sugar from the factories, but when the wind blew in from the sea it smelt sweet and tangy, as though someone had sliced open a lemon.

Their landlady was Rose Mayer, a German woman. She smoked cigars like a man and she was tall, with wild honey-coloured hair that she tied flowers and feathers into, and her skin was the colour of honey too. Ellen thought she was the most beautiful woman she had ever seen, and hoped Samuel hadn't noticed how lovely she was. The house was full of flowers and candles and ornate brass lamps, and instruments lay randomly in corners – a harpsichord, a violin, a flute. Rose Mayer liked parties.

Samuel found work in the kitchen of a fine dining restaurant near Market Street, and Ellen cleaned for Rose. It was nothing like working for the dour Mrs Watkins and her brood of children: this house was filled with song and laughter. Guests came and went, people from all over the world; seamen and salesmen and speculators and adventurers, people escaping, people searching, all of them with stories and secrets.

This was a city of life and of death: Samuel told her about the bars which were run by Shanghaiers, where drunk men were drugged or knocked unconscious and sold as crew to departing ships. You could wake up and find yourself in Shanghai, he said. There were places where you dare not go unless you wanted to risk a slit throat. But it was a city Ellen loved. In the evenings as the sky dimmed and wisps of fog blew in, she and Samuel sat on the wooden balcony of their small room and watched the stretches of swamp and the soft humps of dune. On his days off they'd browse the bookshop in Montgomery Street, with its smoky-sweet scent of paper, and afterwards they'd go to the pier to eat salty clams on the waterfront, or fresh fish cooked over charcoal, or to North Beach for tangy wild yeast sourdough.

'I'm liking this town,' said Samuel. They were sitting by

the choppy sea eating aromatic steamed Chinese dumplings they'd bought from a street vendor. Two sea lions flailed on the wharf, one gleaming and sleek, the other enormous and ancient with one milky eye and spiky black lion-hair around his face. Seagulls yelled and swooped as workers from the restaurants threw fish-heads for them.

'I wouldn't mind sticking around here a while.'

Ellen liked it too, but she wondered when she would get tired of the ground feeling too steady under her feet. At night she always dreamed she was back on the *Mary Alice*.

'I been putting me a little money aside. Thinking of maybe buying a house up in the hills.'

He looked at her to gauge her reaction.

'Nothing fancy. Just a small place with a yard and a swing for the children.'

The children. He never asked directly why after all this time, there was still no child. And because he never asked, she never told him: there will never be one. Even though she knew it was what he wanted most in all the world.

'But if we were out of town you'd have to walk a long way to work,' she said.

'Been thinking about that too. About having a little bar selling food and ale on the front porch.'

Food establishments were springing up all over town, both

for the rich and the not so rich. Ellen nodded. He could see she was unsure.

'Just thinking about it,' he said.

A small dog risked his life by darting to snatch a fish-head, and the sea lions flapped and roared at the sky. Ellen put her arm through Samuel's.

'If we decide to stay,' she said.

*

Rose asked Ellen to prepare the house for a party: the first of many, Ellen was to discover.

She didn't know what to expect – parties hadn't been a feature of her life back home. She brushed cobwebs from chandeliers, shook rugs out of the window, swept the stairs, fetched dusty bottles of wine and brandy and bourbon from the cellar. She squeezed lemons into jugs to make lemonade, put flowers in vases and arranged cut-glass goblets on tables laid with French lace cloths.

She sat on her bed listening to the house fill with voices and felt apprehensive. But then she heard Samuel's voice among the strangers, so she checked her hair in the mirror and went downstairs.

There were women who were as flamboyant as Rose, and languorous men who looked as though they needed a good meal and a dose of sunshine. Someone was playing scales on the piano. Rose grabbed Ellen's arm and said, 'Come and meet my friend Ravi. He's a very good writer.'

Ravi, a Middle-Eastern man with a long, serious face, was talking to Samuel on the balcony. He shook Ellen's hand sadly when Rose introduced them, and immediately returned to his conversation with Samuel, which was about literature. Ellen had nothing to say in these conversations: for her there was nothing much to say about a book. She hated *Jane Eyre* because she couldn't have stood being in the same room as the dreadful Mr Rochester for more than a minute. She loved *Moby Dick* because of the sea and the beautiful whale. Rose brought her a goblet of wine, which she gulped to blur her shyness, and watched the party – artists, writers, musicians, sailors, wanderers – these were Rose's friends who gathered to talk, drink, argue and dance.

A woman started singing, her voice rising above the hubbub. The song was Irish, about a sailor leaving his love behind. She had red hair piled on top of her head and pink-painted cheeks. Ellen got lost in her song, in her high, tremulous voice, because it reminded her of Mammy singing to her as a child, beautiful songs about loss and heartbreak.

The woman noticed Ellen watching her and when she'd finished and the clapping had died down she made her way towards the crowd towards her.

'Are you Irish?' the woman asked.

'My mother is.'

'Ah,' said the woman. 'You see, I recognise an Irish beauty when I see one.' She traced the shape of Ellen's face with her finger before wandering off, sipping wine and smiling at something inside her head.

Later there was more music – some men playing sea-jigs

on fiddles, and Ellen had supped enough wine to be able to join Samuel in a dance. But she felt overwhelmed by these unknown, confident people. Over Samuel's shoulder she watched a woman in a man's suit argue with a man in a man's suit, and a tiny little man spinning round and round, eyes closed and arms in the air, as though in a trance.

'There are some very strange people here,' she whispered to Samuel, and she felt his warm breath as he laughed into her hair.

'Can we go to bed?' she whispered.

He stood back and smiled at her, and by the relief on his face she saw that he felt the same. They slipped out, and as they ascended the stairs they saw Ravi entering Rose's bedroom, heard a woman's laughter from inside. Ellen gripped Samuel's hand and giggled, and they went to bed and dozed to the sound of music and laughter late into the night.

In the morning Ellen flung open the windows to air the house, which smelt of smoke and sweat and bourbon. She saw Rose going down the front steps on her way into town. A passing neighbour stopped and snapped loudly, 'Whore!'

'Oh, I'm not a whore,' said Rose. 'I sleep with men for pleasure, not money.' And she lifted her skirts free of the muddy road and went on her way.

Ellen leaned on the windowsill and watched the scandalised neighbour, watched Rose, watched the city and the dunes beyond and the dark lines of the ships' masts sketched against the sea. She felt the sea wind as the lace curtains breathed against her. Later that afternoon she wrote to Mammy. She didn't tell her she thought she would never come home.

Chapter 20

A Visit

1885

'Come quickly,' called Rose, grabbing Ellen's hand. They ran down the stairs, Rose laughing, Ellen saying, 'What? What is it?'

Standing in the hallway were two people, a man and a woman. The man was a little dishevelled and bearded …

Bright! Ellen jumped down the last two steps and ran into his arms. My brother. My hairy bear. That familiar musty smell.

She released him, looked at the woman, who was slight and olive-skinned, vibrant as a flower, with eyes dark as beads.

'My wife, Mona,' said Bright. And the woman stepped forward and gripped Ellen's hand and said, 'I am very pleased to meet you.' Her voice sing-song and accented.

'Your wife?'

There was so much to know, but so much to do, too. Rose took Bright and Mona to their room and Ellen ran out to tell Samuel, down the windy streets scented with Chinese food, dodging horses and carts who sploshed mud onto her skirts and rowdy miners who called out to her. Past woodyards and foundries, shoemakers, fur shops, denim overall factories, to the restaurant where she peered into the window at the rich people dining, at the gold-painted pillars and the candlelight reflected in the bottles of champagne and Madeira. Samuel told her they ate so much they burst out of their expensive clothes, the waiters clearing up the scattered buttons at the end of the night. And in the booths, hidden behind heavy velvet curtains, ladies dined with gentlemen who were not their husbands.

A waiter, smart and bow-tied, noticed her and came to the door and she told him: tell my husband to hurry home; we have special visitors.

In a steaming kitchen Rose and Ellen prepared a feast of clam chowder, roast beef with lima beans, baked apples and jugs of beer. Samuel arrived home, hugged Bright, his old friend, and greeted Mona, and they all sat down to eat at the big wooden kitchen table.

Conversations cut across one another, everyone was so excited and wanting to know everything, but the main story of the night, told by Bright and Mona who sat touching shoulders, was the story of how they met when his ship docked in Naples.

'I saw her selling lemons at the port. She was the loveliest woman I ever saw.'

'I was with my mother on our stall and I looked up and saw a man who looked just like a bear. I love bears. I had to have him.'

Ellen laughed. Bear had always been her name for him. Hairy Bear.

'So I left the stall and ran after him with my angry Mama calling after me, *Mona! Mona! Ritorno!*'

Like a book, thought Ellen. She imagined Mona running through a flap of panicked chickens, lemons rolling from her basket, people turning to stare. Not like her and Samuel. Their courtship had been quiet, conducted over coffee, just a question and an answer.

Bright and Mona were married in a small whitewashed Italian church two weeks later, without the blessing of her furious parents, and then she ran away to sea with him.

Samuel laughed. 'Why do women follow us to sea?' he joked.

'Because the sea is freedom,' said Rose, serious.

'Do you think Mammy fell in love like that?' wondered Ellen. 'Or was her marriage just a practical thing?'

'Ah, Mammy,' said Bright, glancing at Ellen, then Mona. 'We will never know.'

'I haven't met your mama yet,' said Mona.

'She what we call back home *bewitch*,' said Samuel. 'Crazy. But a good woman. She'll be happy for you.'

Later Samuel and Bright sang sea-shanties in their lovely low voices, and Rose accompanied them on a fiddle, and Mona and Ellen danced, laughing, swinging one other round and round.

'I really like her,' Ellen whispered to Bright. Mona was mesmeric with her bright eyes, her slender gesticulating hands.

There was no hint, not then, of the illness that would follow.

*

Those lovely days. They ate oysters by the sea with the wind whipping their faces. They rode the ornate and rattling cable cars up and down the hills of the town, laughing like children on a fairground ride. They picnicked in the shade of fragrant eucalyptus trees on the banks of a mountain lake.

'How come you stayed here so long?' asked Bright. Mona lay with her head on his lap sucking the juice from the wild strawberries that they had picked earlier.

'You've got to settle somewhere,' said Samuel. Flies buzzed lazily and butterflies flitted the flowers. A swan came in to land on the lake, its feet grabbing at the air before breaking the blue surface.

'Not me,' said Bright and Mona laughed, reached up and put a strawberry in his mouth. 'I'm going to keep on going.'

'As long as you take me with you,' Mona said.

'I have me a plan,' said Samuel. 'This place is as good as any. Better than some. And the people here, they love their food, and not just the rich people. I want to buy me a little bar and sell beer and food. Just simple food, made with love.'

Ellen breathed in the scent of the eucalyptus trees. I never knew a tree could smell like this, she thought. He has been all over the world and seen so much. There is still so much undiscovered for me.

But he didn't have the money saved yet. There was time for both.

Chapter 21

Flatbread

1885

'I want you to take me shopping,' Mona said.

It was a beautiful day, sultry, sunlight slanting in across the floors, bored flies idling against the windows. Ellen and Mona took parasols and a basket and walked down the hill towards the port. Mona was excited, chatty. She loved everything here – the bustle, the tall buildings, the elegant plazas with their palm trees, the aromatic coffee shops, the coloured paper lanterns hanging above the doors of the Chinese shops.

'*Bellissimo!*' she exclaimed, crouching down to pinch the cheeks of two children dressed in silk robes. A man came out of the darkness of the shop and she chatted to him in Italian and in English, about how beautiful his children were, how beautiful the lanterns were. She called Ellen – who was hanging back – to bring the purse, and she bought some mushrooms, a floret of broccoli, some fat red tomatoes and a bunch of oregano.

'I am cooking tonight,' she said, waving goodbye to the man and his children. She bought a bag of flour and yeast from a baker and then met an Italian street vendor with baskets hanging from his shoulders. After an excited, animated conversation she bought a bottle of olive oil. Finally they went to the pier where she bought a basket of small herring, fresh off the boat. With everyone she was the same; exuberant and talkative, and Ellen, her head spinning a little, wished she could be like Mona, so unselfconscious; a beautiful whirlwind of a girl.

They sat drinking sarsaparilla and looking over the fidgety blue water. Behind them the town rose steeply up, and on the waterfront ships rocked beside the wharfs. Sweat-shiny horses waited for their carts to be filled, heads low, tails lashing irritably against the flies. Fishing boats came and went across the bay hauling nets, clouds of screaming seabirds swooping round them.

'Tell me what Bright was like when he was a little boy,' Mona said.

Ellen thought a moment. She remembered the smell of him, salty-sweet; a scent of the river and the sky. Crouching in the gutter with him, sailing paper boats in muddy rainwater rivulets. Another boy reeling backwards, bloody-nosed, punched by Bright for pulling Ellen's hair. Bright giving her a piggy-back over a stream, her knees gripping his waist, her hands clutching his dog-dusty hair.

'He was kind,' she said. 'He looked after me.'

And Mona smiled.

Back in the house they flung open the windows in the kitchen to let the sun and the breeze in, and Mona made flatbreads, garnished them with tomatoes, broccoli, mushrooms, sliced herring and oregano. Then she put them in the bread oven to bake, and when Samuel came home from work they all sat down to eat Mona's delicious flatbreads, all the way from Naples.

The next morning Bright and Mona left on a ship for Melbourne, and Ellen cried and held onto both of them and didn't want to let them go.

Chapter 22

A Letter

1887

Samuel sent part of his cook's wages to his mother in Barbados every month, and she had used it to leave her labouring job and move to a little house on the north-east of the island. She wrote letters telling him about it and Samuel, sitting on the bed in his vest after work, read parts of them to Ellen.

'She can see the sea from the porch. All sweet and briny.'

'She working on her vegetable patch.'

'She got coconut trees and bananas. And ackee. She worked so hard to give me an education, for me to have a better life than she had. She deserves this now.'

'Did she have only one child?' asked Ellen. He had never mentioned siblings.

'No, she had more. All gone.'

'Gone? Where?' To sea, like him, scattered around the world?

'In the ground. None of them grew past being babies.'

Ellen stared at him.

'Amos, Sol and Eve.'

The naming of them made it worse.

'Your poor mother.'

He caught her horror: all those babies. Lost in the earth. He swiftly changed the subject.

'She wants to meet you.'

*

Ellen was stripping a guest's bed. The man had been a drunkard – there were whisky bottles under the bed and the sheets were urine-stained. She was exasperated – how could people let themselves get into that state? She heard Samuel's footsteps on the stairs. They were hurried, more urgent than usual. She paused, called: 'I'm in here.' He appeared in the doorway, made a face at the mess in the room and then held out a piece of paper.

'What is it?'

'Have a look.'

She took it. It was a ticket, a passage to Bridgetown, Barbados, on a ship called *Sea Song*. The ticket had her name on it. She looked at him, not understanding.

'I got me a job on that ship.'

'But your job here …'

'There will be others. I want to introduce you to my mother.'

Rose was excited, gave Ellen some light frocks and a parasol and a hat with silk flowers sown around its brim. 'It'll be hot. And you'll need to look pretty for your mother-in-law!' She promised to keep their room for their return. But Ellen wondered if they would return: she was excited to start travelling the world again.

Chapter 23

Island

1887

Old Joe had told her there was such a thing as a bad ship, and the *Sea Song* was one of them. She was old – shabby, squat and sullen with none of the elegance of the *Mary Alice*. The captain was sloppy and half the crew drunkards. As they followed the coast of Argentina a fever swept the ship leaving twelve passengers and three crew dead, including the woman in the berth above Ellen in steerage. Samuel had insisted Ellen would be more comfortable in a proper bunk but it was dreadful, with a stench of overflowing toilets and clouds of flies and rats running over her face in the night. Ellen spent a night cooling the poor woman's brow and moistening her lips, as the woman bucked and kicked against the sickness, her skin red as dolphin meat, foaming at the mouth and screaming as though the devil was inside her. It reminded Ellen of something …

Then the woman died suddenly, mid-scream and staring, appalled, at something on the ceiling just above Ellen's head.

Ellen made the sign of the cross and whispered, 'In the name of the Father and the Son and of the Holy Spirit Amen,' before running out.

'I am not going back in those berths,' she told Samuel.

And then she was ill herself, coughing, her ribs feeling as though they had cracked in two. She cried: 'I'm going to die too!' and the doctor came and listened to her chest and said she had a pleurisy, the ship's damp in her lungs. For days she lay still, breathing shallowly, each breath a stab in her chest and her body drenched in sweat, whispering to her rosary, whispering to Mammy who sat by her bed staring at her with unblinking eyes.

The galley was a bad-tempered place – fights broke out and Samuel was sombre. There was none of the camaraderie and the joking, the singing or storytelling or card-playing or sea-watching that was life on the *Mary Alice*. Ellen was scared of the dead and dying people and of the drunken crew, so she stayed below deck, tucked in a corner of the galley, close to Samuel. She didn't even go up on deck to watch the approach to Rio de Janeiro, where they docked to offload the bodies.

But eventually, they arrived. Samuel woke her from an unpleasant, musty dream about the dead woman that lingered just out of the reach of her memory.

'We approaching Bridgetown. Come.'

She swung out of the hammock, reluctant, and followed him, but what she saw chased the aftertaste of the dream right away. Because as soon as she walked on deck she entered another dream, the one she had had since she was tiny, flying over a gleaming navy sea with a thousand stars reflected, flying to where Bright was. She knew this place.

They leaned on the rail. Even in the darkness the air was so humid she could taste it, its warmth inside her chest melting away the last of the pleurisy. As the *Sea Song* approached the soft gaslights of Bridgetown, she could smell the island, a sweet saltiness and a scent of warm earth. And she could hear its song above the thrum of the ship's engine: the chanting of the frogs, as lovely and discordant as church bells.

Then dawn broke and the sky burned rose pink. The sea and the island filled with colour as though someone was pouring paint into it, and she felt the colours pour into her too.

Samuel smiled at her. This was what he had wanted her to see.

She was glad to leave that dreadful ship but as she disembarked and Samuel left her to fetch their sea-chest she felt shy. She was used to port bustle – shouting men, women with baskets on their heads, donkeys, horses, a skit of escaped piglets. But here, hers was the only white face. Elegant women with bright white dresses and parasols passed by and as they glanced at her she turned away, self-conscious.

Is this how Samuel feels? she wondered.

The crew headed into Bridgetown to board but Samuel found them a room in a quieter area, in a colonial building on the edge of town. The landlady was a tall woman, polite but unsmiling, her hair wrapped in a gold coloured scarf. Samuel stood in the doorway making the arrangements for their stay as Ellen looked around the shuttered room, and the woman glanced over Samuel's shoulder to get a curious look at her, this white woman who, after weeks on a ship, looked like a guttersnipe.

The woman brought bowls of water, and left. Ellen sat on the bed trying to tug pins from her salty hair.

'What will people think of me?' It hadn't mattered before, in the other ports; she had never cared what anyone thought. But here it mattered, enough to leave a knot in the pit of her stomach. Ellen, close to tears.

What will *she* think of me?

'Hush, hush,' said Samuel, pulling her hands away. He teased the pins out, pulled the tangles out strand by strand, until she was calmer and her hair smooth enough to brush. Then he unhooked her dirty old dress and washed her back with soft fingers, with cool water.

They dressed in their best clothes, Ellen in a pink dress that Rose had given her and a hat with silk flowers, Samuel in a grey jacket and Panama hat, a blue scarf knotted around his neck. They adjusted one another's clothes – the neckline, the hemline, the jaunt of the hat, until they were just right. Ellen kissed Samuel's cheek.

'You are handsome.'

'And you are beautiful.'

*

Seymour and his donkey, Freddie, took them north in a cart.

Ellen sat in the back, her parasol shading her from the sun. Samuel sat up front with Seymour, chatting. Seymour was old but as sinewy as a boy, with sea-green smile-creased eyes. Ellen gathered during the chat that there were people they both knew, friends of friends, cousins of cousins, but she didn't try and keep up.

102

They travelled along the coast road for a bit, the cart rocking with the donkey's tap-tap rhythm. The sea was the colour of washed glass, fork-tailed seabirds diving. Palm trees trailed their tendrils onto pale sand and solitary fishermen sat dreaming on rocks.

She heard the voice of the sea: hush, it said. Hush.

They turned inland, onto a dusty track, through villages of painted wooden houses. Samuel turned to Ellen to point out the houses' ornate fretwork, their pretty shingle roof tiles.

'My father was a carpenter. Made things like that.'

Dogs pretended to guard their homes as they passed, hurling themselves towards the cart before giving up and dropping down into the hot dust. Old men sat in the shade of palms and banana trees playing dominoes, and pigeons sheltered under benches, open-beaked. As the cart rattled across a wooden bridge over a pond, women who were scrubbing clothes on the bleached rocks turned to watch them, arms up to shade their eyes.

Ellen saw a toad on a boulder sitting as still as a statue; white egrets in a freshly ploughed field; a hummingbird feeding from a red flower.

They arrived at a small village in the north of the island. There was a smell of fried fish coming from somewhere and the air was full of the flutey voices of birds. The sea exhaled down below, sliding over coral, and the rugged Atlantic coastline was soft with sea spray.

'Wait here,' said Samuel, and Ellen's stomach constricted.

103

Samuel went to talk to a woman who had been watching them from her front porch. Is that her? Ellen wondered. Seymour took a knife from his pocket, cut a coconut from a tree and sliced the shell.

'Make you strong,' Seymour said, and rolled up his sleeves to show her his sinewy arms.

More people came out of their houses, gathered round Samuel. Seymour sliced a piece of coconut shell and gave it to Ellen.

'A spoon.'

Inside the coconut it was translucent, like jellyfish.

In the cluster of people there was fast chatter, pointing, shaking of heads.

'Clears the skin,' said Seymour to Ellen, and then giggled, indicating that she was using the spoon back to front. She turned the spoon round, tasted the sweet fruit and nodded to Seymour: yes, she liked it. A lizard sashayed across the track in front of the cart and disappeared into long grass. The donkey shifted on his knuckly legs and sighed.

Samuel was walking back to them. Ellen waited. But he didn't speak to her. Climbing back into the cart beside Seymour he said something that Ellen didn't catch, and Seymour clicked the donkey's reins and they headed back the way they had come.

Ellen turned, saw the group of neighbours watching them go.

*

The donkey-cart rocked back through the island, this time passing between tall fields of singing sugar cane. The donkey twitched his ears and tail against small insistent flies. Ellen leant forward, tapped Samuel on the shoulder.

'What's happened? Where is your mother?'

'She doesn't live there.'

'But she must do. You sent money.'

'I sent it to the General Post Office. Not to a house.'

Windmills spun, indolent, and the sugar cane bowed in the breeze.

And then Seymour pulled the donkey up.

'This the best place to stop,' he said. Samuel got out of the cart and Ellen stood up too. Samuel hesitated before helping her down, as though he did not want her to come.

'Take your time,' said Seymour, before settling himself down under the drooping fonds of an ancient bearded fig tree and pulling his hat down over his eyes.

Samuel, followed by Ellen, walked through cane higher than their heads. The lovely rustle of it.

The field opened onto a manicured lawn, and at the far end of the lawn stood a large bay-windowed Jacobean house.

'What is this place?'

'This is where I grew up.'

Ellen started to follow Samuel across the lawn, but he turned and said, sharp, 'Wait here.'

She found a shaded bench and sat down surrounded by hibiscus, orchids, roses, mango, avocado and breadfruit trees. The garden ran down to another field of whispering sugar cane and beyond that a sliver of sea of the deepest turquoise. From the open windows of the house she could hear women's laughter, the rise and fall of the servants' voices. Strange birds sang in a woodland of dark, tall trees behind the house. And through the trees, half-hidden, a row of painted wooden huts.

She thought, he was a little boy here, in these scented gardens. She imagined him running, climbing trees. What a lovely little boy he must have been.

A cockerel crowed.

Even in the shade she was hot, little streams of sweat dribbling from under her hat. She fanned herself with her hands. She could hear the tinkle of teacups from the cool of the house.

Then, through the languorous afternoon, a burst of raised voices, men shouting. Samuel appeared from the back of the house. Ellen stood up. Samuel strode towards her but he passed without looking at her, his eyes hard, blank, reflecting nothing. She hitched up her skirt and ran after him.

'Samuel, Samuel, what is it?'

He kept on walking. The whispering cane bent before him,

106

then regrouped above his head. At the bottom of the field, watched by a white man on a horse, were a group of labourers – men in sweat-soaked vests with stone-sculpted arms swiping large machetes at the cane's feet; women, their heads wrapped in wreaths of cloth, hauling the heavy bunches of cane onto carts. The carts were hitched to bow-headed horses, shivers darting across their wet coats, tails slapping the flies away. Barefoot children sucked at sugar cane leaves.

How can they work in this heat? Ellen wondered.

The white man caught his horse up when he saw Samuel, circled him as though to stop him, but Samuel walked straight on without seeing him and the man pulled his horse up and just watched him go. Something about the way he walked made him unapproachable even to a foreman.

Ellen caught up with him on the dusty lane. Grabbed his arm. His eyes still didn't see her, were elsewhere, and she was afraid.

'What is it? Where's your mother?'

'Gone,' he said.

'Gone dead?'

'Gone dead.'

*

And then Samuel disappeared.

When they arrived back at the boarding house he spoke to

the landlady briefly and then left Ellen alone. She pulled open the shutters and watched the sea, and waited. And waited.

Sometime later the landlady's daughter brought her a bowl of rice and peas and a glass of lemonade. The girl was beautiful, tall and dark, maybe eighteen years old, with an easier smile than her mother. Ellen had the feeling she knew where Samuel was, but didn't dare to ask.

The night in Barbados fell quickly, the sky turning the colour of irises, then black. Still Samuel didn't come back. Ellen stripped to her petticoat and slept a frightened hot sleep to the sound of frogs and crickets and mournful night-time birds.

The sun woke her in the morning, sharp in her eyes. She wondered why she felt weighed down, and then she remembered: Joanna was dead, Samuel was gone, and she was alone.

What if he never came back? What would she do, an abandoned white woman in a strange country? She didn't even have Joanna to run to.

He'll come back, he'll come back, she said to herself, to calm her dread.

The landlady's daughter visited again with a breakfast of fried fish and rice. Ellen felt sick and didn't want to eat it but didn't want to seem rude. She ate, she watched the sea, she watched the sky. The air in the room was choking.

In the afternoon she put her boots on and went out.

She walked through some scrubby bushes and down to the sea. There was no one about except some children playing, far away along the beach. Her boots crunched in the hot pale sand.

The weather was changing and there were rainclouds across the sea, so dark it looked as though someone had drawn a charcoal line across the horizon. The sea was grey and choppy but when the waves rose the water underneath was an astonishing blue.

'The colour is aqua,' said a voice behind her. 'Means water.'

Ellen turned. The landlady's daughter stood there, smiling.

'Aqua,' repeated Ellen. It was a lovely word.

'Your husband said I have to look after you,' said the girl. Ellen turned away from her.

'How nice of him.'

They watched the wash of the waves for a moment, then the girl bent and unlaced her boots. She smiled at Ellen, hitched up her skirt and walked into the sea.

'Having me a sea-bath,' she said.

Ellen watched her wading in, watched as the turquoise belly of the wave broke around her.

Then she sat down and pulled her boots off too.

She remembered the shock of leaping into the river when

she was a child, but this water, sucking at her toes, was warm, soft.

'What's your name?' she called to the girl.

'Rosalind.'

Ellen walked deeper in, holding her skirt up. The water was as clear as glass and little yellow and black fish darted around her ankles. Deeper; the water lapped at her thighs and she let her skirt go and it floated round her like a fan. Large black crabs trundled across rocks, clumsy as mechanical toys. She followed Rosalind until the water was up to their stomachs, and they laughed as waves spat at their breasts, at their faces, and they watched the rainclouds race in towards the island.

'You feel better?' asked Rosalind.

'Yes,' said Ellen. The sea had washed something out of her, left her clean inside.

'Then we better go before the rain comes in,' said Rosalind. 'And before my mama whips my behind.'

Back in the room Ellen took off her wet clothes and got into bed and dozed, still feeling the motion of the waves around her. And later, when it was night again and the frogs were singing she heard the door click open and Samuel slipped into bed beside her, warm against her back, smelling of whisky and smoke. They lay together listening to the rain-drip on the leaves outside, and she felt hot tears against her skin.

'Hush,' she whispered. 'Everything's all right. Hush.'

She never asked him where he had gone. She assumed it wasn't to a woman, who would have asked him things he wanted to bury, but to men; men who talked about everything and about nothing. The next day they went fishing and he seemed calm, and she remembered when Daddy died, that sometimes it had felt like the most natural thing in the world and that she must have known he'd die on that day. And then she would be overcome by panic: this could not have happened. It was impossible for Daddy not to be in the world any more: no-no-no-no-no.

Today, Samuel didn't seem to be panicked. But he was silent.

The sea was as still as a lake with silver flying fish leaping, graceful as birds. Samuel hauled in a small blue barracuda that writhed and snapped its monstrous teeth and then lay gasping on the floor of the boat until its eyes turned glassy.

'Small enough to eat,' said Samuel. 'The big ones make you sick.' It was the first thing he'd said for hours.

They rowed back to shore and Samuel made a fire on the beach in the shade of the palm trees and fried the fish, and they ate it with their fingers, pulling hot flesh from bone, while monkeys shrieked at them from the trees. Then a wind swept in from the sea bringing hot dark clouds that were fat with rain, and they ran for the shelter of the boarding house. Ellen wanted to ask him how he felt but she was afraid of his silence; she couldn't find a way through.

Chapter 24

Kadooment

1887

It rained for days, huge humid drops spilling from leaves. Geckos and snails the size of mice crept into their room for shelter. Outside, the dusty track became a torrent of rushing, splashing mud.

When Daddy died, Ellen ran to Mammy, wanting to be told it hadn't happened, it was a dream, that Daddy would come back. Mammy went howling her grief to the priest and shut her daughter out. Bright ran away from his grief by escaping on a ship. But Ellen had never seen grief like Samuel's before, entombed and silent. They sat in their room for days, and for days he barely spoke.

And then, the day the rain stopped at last, someone came to visit. Ellen peered through the door of their room and watched as Samuel spoke amiably to a young man; he even heard him laugh. Then the man went away and Samuel came back into the room.

'Who was that?'

'An old friend from the plantation.'

'What did he want?'

'To invite us to a party.'

'A party?'

Ellen saw his face start to close again.

'We're not going.'

Ellen looked through the shutters. Outside, the mud was gleaming, steam rising from it as the sun blazed down from an astonishing blue sky. She turned to face Samuel.

'Yes we are.'

He opened his mouth to speak but she held a hand up to stop him.

'I am not sitting inside these four walls until our ship arrives. I'm sick of it, Samuel Jordan. We are going to the party.'

*

She remembers this night now in fragments, pieces of a kaleidoscope, maybe because of the mugs of bittersweet drink, which burned her throat and sent her head flying from her body.

She remembers the air smelling of burning sugar and roasting meat and distant music coming closer; drums and fiddles and banjos and whistles. A dancing procession silhouetted against a turquoise sky. Masked men on stilts, and men dressed as women with exaggerated stuffed breasts and bottoms, and women with flowers in their hair. A man with the head of a donkey, and a real donkey with ribbons flying from his mane pulling a cart heavy with cane.

She remembers Samuel taking her hand and joining the masquerade.

An ox spinning above a fire, its carcass reddening and spitting. Pieces of coloured cloth blowing from the windows of the house. She remembers white people watching and clapping from the terrace but not joining in. She remembers a tiny old man with one arm, skin creased as paper and blackened teeth embracing Samuel.

'I'm sorry for your mother,' he said. And more people joined in and spoke of her: Joanna was kind. Joanna sang beautiful songs in the morning. Joanna made the best pie. Joanna was, Joanna was, Joanna was; it was like there were pieces of her dancing in the air with the hot ash.

She remembers an elderly white man approaching Samuel through the throng, and Samuel shaking off her hand and going to speak with him, and the man holding out something to Samuel, insistent, that Samuel didn't take. Samuel stepping back, shaking his head, then walking away. She remembers the elderly man standing still as a stone among all the dancers before disappearing. And she remembers she didn't ask what had taken place.

The frogs started to sing, a million tiny voices, and a figure made of cane and dressed in a white suit and top hat was set ablaze, moths flying in the flames. The music became louder, more frenetic, and one by one couples old and young danced while everyone else made a circle round them, whooping and stamping, their bodies loose and supple, even the old people

114

moving in a way that Ellen could not imagine human bodies being able to do. When it was their turn Samuel pulled her into the centre and she tried to dance but she couldn't; she could dance a waltz and a polka but this dancing was nothing like that, and she tried, and she couldn't, and she laughed and everyone else laughed and she felt foolish, and as though she would never be able to put the pieces of herself back together again. And with her head full of rum on this steamy night on this beautiful island with her husband, that was all right.

Chapter 25

Wicked

1887

Rose had kept their room for them as promised: the house was large enough for her to make her living with the other rooms.

On the evening of their return she came rushing up with a carafe of bourbon and a box of cigars, flowers in her hair, flamboyant. She kissed them both before sitting down, pouring three glasses of bourbon.

'Tell me. Tell me everything.'

Samuel took a cigar and lit it. It was a cool evening, the city huddled under yellow fog.

'Samuel's mother died,' Ellen said, to save him from saying it.

'I'm so sorry. What happened?'

Ellen did not expect him to answer, because he hadn't told her anything, and since she thought he didn't want to talk about it she hadn't asked. But he inhaled a mouthful of smoke, exhaled again, and spoke.

He said the money he had been sending had not been enough. Because the price of sugar was dropping, her employer and owner of the plantation who was also her landlord, had kept the rents up and cut wages, so that she could not afford to move. She didn't want to tell her son that his money was going for nothing, so she invented the little house in St Lucy. She was hoping that by the time he visited her she may have put enough of Samuel's money aside to have made it true. But before she could manage it, she died.

'How?'

'She was sick with a fever. But she wasn't allowed time off until the crop was cut. She fainted and fell under the wheels of a cart.'

Ellen thought about the letters Samuel had read to her, all the little details. The smell of the sea, the vegetable patch, the kindly neighbours. In inventing that house Joanna had loved it. For a long moment no one said anything. And then Rose said, 'Lord. Some wicked things have been done just so people can taste that sweet stuff.'

'The plantation owner tried to pay me as an apology,' said Samuel, and Ellen remembered, in that hazy night, the elderly white man.

'But no money in the world is enough. Slavery is gone in name only.'

He looked at Ellen. 'Did you see the man with one arm?'

Ellen nodded; he was very old and thin as a bird, the empty arm of one shirt sleeve tied and swinging.

'He got his arm caught in the cane-roller. The overseer cut it off with a machete so they could continue the sugar production. The sugar is worth more than we are.'

Ellen looked at him and saw the pain in his expression, a rawness that she had never seen in him. Why didn't I know? she thought. Why didn't I ask?

And then Rose said, 'My grandmother was a slave. In Jamaica.'

'Are you serious?' Samuel smiled at this: a connection between them. Ellen looked at her, at her coily hair, her wide mouth and honey skin, and saw it, the ghost of her Jamaican grandmother in her lovely face.

'My grandfather was her owner. She was a clever woman. There are not many ways for a woman to get ahead in the world, yet alone a slave woman, but she found a way.'

'Some do,' said Samuel, and there was a silence. 'And some don't. Slavery is something you hold inside your bones. It's not so easy to get rid of, even when they say it's over.'

He drained his glass. Rose filled it again. He looked at Ellen.

'At the bottom of the Atlantic sea,' he said, 'there is a garden of bones. They are the bones of Africans who were taken on the Middle Passage.'

'The Middle Passage?'

'A journey from the West of Africa to the Caribbean and the Americas. The Africans were chained to one another in the hold, men, women, children. Some died of disease, or thirst, or from beatings. Were thrown overboard. Some managed to escape their chains and jump into the ocean, and some starved themselves to death rather than complete this journey and face what was at the end of it.'

Ellen had heard of slavery, but only in the way that it was an abstract thing that had happened in the past. She knew that slavery was bad and Great Britain was good because they had abolished it. It occurred to her now that they wouldn't have had to abolish it if they hadn't participated in it in the first place.

'I remember, when I was a little boy, seeing a man washing in the stream and his back was criss-crossed with scars, looked like snakes slithering over him. And I asked my mother, what is that. And she said, that's why you don't go playing in the woods on your own. There are tigers in there.' He laughed. Then he stopped.

'Only when I got older, I realised, there are no tigers in those woods.'

A burst of raised voices somewhere in the city, a dog barking. Then silence again. Mist breathed on them.

'What was your grandmother's name?' Ellen asked Rose. She wanted something, some piece of information to be able to be able to access these women whose lives she could not fathom.

'Hope.'

Samuel was looking over the soft hills. 'And this country

is no paradise,' said Samuel. 'Lynchings and strange fruit and stuff. Those devils in white sheets burning crosses.'

'No paradise if you're Chinese, or Mexican, or Native, either,' said Rose.

Ellen sipped the bourbon, felt it burning her throat as it went down, as she listened to Rose and Samuel talking about things she'd had no idea about.

Later when they went to bed she pressed her hands against Samuel's chest, wanting to push through his skin to his heart and hold it in her arms.

How are human beings so wicked, she wondered.

*

Now, all these years later, she lies in bed, pains shooting through her bones like daggers of ice. In the back room Louis and Mary are listening to the wireless. She imagines Mary's head, bent, darning holes in the children's clothes, and Louis smoking, watching the wisps rise, listening to the voices on the wireless. What horrors are they telling of now, she wonders. She knows that across Europe something terrible is spreading, like ink spilt on a map.

And then she remembers a wedding party in San Francisco. A Mexican friend of Samuel's was getting married, and they were invited to the party. There would be dancing all night. They often went dancing in one of the little bars down by the pier, but this, she was told, was different.

'The Mexicans can dance like no one else,' said Rose as

she ran her hands along the frocks hanging in her wardrobe, looking for something suitably dazzling for Ellen to wear.

And Rose was right. In a small backyard, to the music of a Mariachi band, they danced polkas and waltzes and tangos. The bride, Constanza, wore a red flowered dress and her white veil flew as her white-suited groom spun her round and round, and a goat turned slowly on a spit, its throat slit like a smile, and the air was scented with the burning sugar that was sprinkled on the fire.

They danced all night and then walked in a procession to the dunes where a picnic was laid out on a blanket; *carne asada*, *tamales*, *dulces*, and wine, more wine. Ellen and Samuel lay eating wild strawberries, watching the sky turn the colour of oysters and listening to waking seabirds.

'After this, they will go back and dance some more,' Samuel told her and she laughed, and rolled into him.

'No! No!'

They walked home, exhausted, in the soft dawn, swaying a little and Ellen leaning against Samuel. Remembering the lovely night she pulled her face to his and kissed him.

'Disgusting!' A woman stood in their way, her hands on her hips. Ellen laughed.

'Aren't we?'

She kissed Samuel again and sashayed past the outraged women, throwing her a mocking glance before turning back to smile at Samuel.

121

But he wasn't smiling and she saw that his pleasure had been wiped away.

And she said nothing.

Wickedness is not just the big things, she thinks now. It is also the small things: the things we don't say. The things we allow.

Chapter 26

Fish

1887

Samuel took her walking in the hills. Down below the town curved around the bay and the lemony air blew in from the ocean. They walked a track that led to the mines, and by the track, set a little back, was a wooden shack.

Samuel pushed the door open and they went inside, to dust dancing in the light through the slatted windows and worm-chewed floorboards.

'What is this place?'

'It's going to be mine.'

'Samuel Jordan, I am not living here. It's not fit for rats.'

A dark shadow scuttered against the wall and Samuel laughed.

'The rats don't agree.'

He gestured around the room. 'This will be the kitchen …'

He pushed open a door at the far end of the room.

'And this the bedroom.'

She walked into the bedroom, coughing with the dust.

'You are teasing me.'

Samuel pulled a slat from the window at the back of the bedroom: some scrubby trees bent sideways, sculpted by sea-wind.

'There is plenty of land. I can build more rooms and still have room for chickens, maybe some goats.'

He took her out to the front of the shack.

'Here I will build a little terrace with a roof, where people can come and eat, and drink.'

'Who will come *here* to eat?'

'Miners on their way to and from work. And when word spreads, other people will come too, because the food will be good and the air here is sweet.'

'Why didn't you tell me?'

'I did.'

'But not that it was going to happen so soon …'

She sat on a log and looked down the hill to the bay.

'There are still so many places I want to travel to.'

'We can employ workers to look after it while we're gone.'

She was silent. It was not much of a quarrel, but it was their first one.

'I'll get it shipshape for you. A coat of paint and some elbow-grease and it'll be a palace,' he said. 'We'll still travel the world.'

'D'you promise?'

'I promise. But we'll have somewhere to come back to. You like it here, don't you?'

She nodded. She imagined them here, cooking together like they did on the *Mary Alice*. Watching the day rise and fade over the sea. And then, when they were tired of the land, heading off on a ship again.

'Have you bought it yet?'

'Not yet. I wanted to show you first.'

'If there's one speck of dust left …'

Samuel laughed. 'No dust.'

He kissed her.

'And now I will take you to the pier to eat fish.'

*

She was getting fat with all that fried fish, her belly and her breasts pushing against her dress.

She dreamed there was a fish swimming inside her. She pushed her fist through the skin and pulled it out, tail first. It had the face of the Chinese Rock Cod with its headlamp eyes and it writhed in her hand, sharp yellow teeth snapping.

Then she started being sick, again and again, crouched over the chamber pot with Rose holding her hair.

Rose was excited. 'You know what this must mean ...'

But no. It couldn't. She had eaten a bad clam. It could only be that. Because a long time ago she had lain in her bed and said a prayer. And it had worked. Even though she had been married three years she still bled every month. No baby had come. No baby would ever come because she had wished it.

'It's not a baby. It can't be. Please don't tell Samuel.'

Rose promised not to but insisted she saw a doctor.

In a clean white room Ellen lay on her back on a raised bed behind a curtain as the doctor, a man with a mournful face, prodded and poked her belly with long thoughtful hands, then held her nipples between his fingers as cautiously as though they were bees. Then he disappeared behind the curtain. Ellen scrambled off the bed, hooking her dress up, pulling her skirts down, and followed him. The doctor had his back to her and was writing something in a notebook.

'Well?' she said.

The doctor turned and looked at her as though he had forgotten who she was.

'Ah,' he said. 'Congratulations Mrs Jordan. You are with child.'

He advised her to drink ginger tea for the sickness, to avoid over-exertion, and to visit again in one month.

Rose was sitting in the waiting room, impatient. Ellen walked past her and out onto the street. It was the same street she had stood on some half an hour before but now it seemed different. Rosy women pushed perambulators past, their fat babies leaning out to stare at her, smiling their terrible smiles. They knew.

Rose took hold of her arm, pulled her round to face her.

'Tell me!'

And Ellen nodded the confirmation.

Crowds jostled them as they walked through the streets, Rose, her arm through Ellen's, chatting.

'I think it's going to be a girl. I'm sure it's going to be a girl. I'm going to teach her the piano before she can walk …'

Her words didn't make any sense to Ellen. Something had been stripped from the world. It was as though she had woken up on another planet.

Then Rose stopped.

'Oh look!'

She was peering into the dusty window of an old shop. She took Ellen's hand and pushed the door, the bell tinkling their arrival. The shop smelled of sawn wood and lavender polish and was filled with ornately carved chairs and tables, sideboards and cupboards. An old man pushed through a curtain at the back. He was small, elfin, wearing a dusty overall.

'Can I help you?'

Then Ellen saw what Rose had been looking at. In the window was a rocking crib in cherry-coloured wood, happy fat cherubs carved into its sides.

'How much is this?' asked Rose.

'Rose, no!'

Rose smiled at her.

'It's a present.'

She turned back to the man. Ellen turned and left the shop. And outside, in the middle of an ordinary busy street, she wept.

Rose rushed after her, wrapped her arms around her. Ellen could smell her lovely scent, which was the same in this new world as it had been in the old one.

'I'm sorry. I've been insensitive. It's too early.'

Ellen shook her head. She wasn't to know, and there was no way to explain.

'You haven't even told Samuel yet. What was I thinking.'

'It's just a shock, that's all.'

'Of course.'

They boarded a horse-bus and Rose held Ellen's hand all the way home. Neither of them spoke. At home Ellen used her sickness as an excuse to go to bed, where she lay in the darkness, her hands pressed against her stomach thinking, leave me. Go.

Later, there were voices in the hallway, footsteps on the stairs. The door creaked open. Samuel approached the bed, looking down at her through the gloom.

'How are you feeling?'

'Fine.'

'Rose say you have something to tell me.'

'I'm going to have a baby.'

She felt his face against hers, his wordless excitement. And she turned away from him to try and shut it out.

Chapter 27

Llewelyn

1872

She is eight years old.

Deep in the night she is woken by footsteps on the stairs, urgent voices, and Mammy in her bedroom sounding strange, moaning oh, oh, oh. Mammy is sick; Mammy needs her. She gets out of bed and goes into the hall. Mammy's bedroom door is ajar, candlelight in the crack. She pushes it open and steps inside. The bedroom is full of people, women, neighbours. They are trying to pull up Mammy to her feet, Mammy who is crawling on all fours and spitting at them, spitting and cursing. Ellen has never heard such words come out of her. It's not Mammy, it can't be, a demon has taken over her. Her face doesn't even look like Mammy: she's red and contorted and ugly. Ellen wants to run but there is nowhere to go, she can't go out into the dark hall, not now that she knows the devils are in the house. A man comes in. The priest, she thinks, he must be. But he's not wearing priest clothes. He has white hair and he is carrying a leather briefcase. He pushes the women out of the way and pulls Mammy up by her shoulders: 'Come on Mrs Jones, behave yourself.' He hoists her onto the bed and she starts screaming, screaming. Mammy is dying; the thing inside her is killing her. The man pushes her onto her back and straps her ankles to the bed bars and lifts up her nightie and Ellen can see, oh Ellen can see something that is not Mammy and there is blood too, so much blood, all down her legs, spreading over the sheets. He orders the women out but he doesn't see Ellen, nobody sees Ellen, she is like a little ghost standing in the corner in her white night-gown.

'Stop making such a fuss, Mrs Jones,' says the man, taking off his jacket. He takes a metal pincers out of his briefcase, like the ones Daddy uses to turn over hot coals on the fire. Is he going to pull the devil out with that? Mammy is bucking on the bed like a horse and the man puts his head down into that terrible place between her legs and Mammy arches her back up and yells, the sound coming from hell itself, and the man rolls his sleeves up, jams his foot against the leg of the bed and starts heaving, as hard as if he's pulling a train from a tunnel. The veins in his arms are plumping fit to burst and he's grunting like a boar with every tug, and Mammy is howling for him to stop please stop but he keeps going, he keeps going until at last he falls backwards.

In between Mammy's legs, lying in the blood, is a blue thing, a jellyfish creature, and Mammy stops screaming and just stares at the ceiling and the man picks the blue thing up and slaps it. Ellen sees a small closed-eye face and a curled hand and then she knows, she knows, and the silence now is the loudest noise of all.

After the birth-death of her baby brother Llewelyn, Ellen climbs into her bed and looks out at the frozen sky and tries to find God there, and whispers, please, let me never ever ever have a baby.

*

Rose found her crying on the balcony.

'What on earth is the matter?'

'You'll think I'm stupid.'

'I won't.'

Rose pulled a chair up, handed her a handkerchief, waited while Ellen blew her nose. Ribbons of rain moved in from the hills.

'I'm afraid.'

'What of?'

'I feel like this thing inside me is … is a monster. And I'm afraid.'

'Oh,' said Rose. 'Well it's probably not a monster, but I don't think you're stupid. I'm sure if I was having a baby I'd feel the same.'

'I never wanted one,' said Ellen, sobbing again. 'But Samuel's so happy, and I can't tell him.'

'He doesn't need to know. We'll get you the best doctor in San Francisco. And I'll look after you. People do have babies, you know.'

Ellen knew. They had dead blue babies that split their bodies open like peaches.

Down below, in the mud-splashed street, they could see

Samuel approaching. When he saw them he held something up to show them. He was smiling.

It was a piece of paper.

Rose rubbed at Ellen's eyes with the handkerchief.

'You'll be all right,' she said. 'We'll all be all right.' And they stood up and waved and clapped at Samuel, who was holding the deeds to the shack.

*

On his days off Samuel worked on the shack, cleaning and painting and sawing, coming home with dusty hair and paint-spattered hands. Rose and Ellen perused the market, buying pieces of French lace and china crockery, and wool for Ellen to crochet blankets with, although Rose said she didn't need to move if she didn't want to.

'You can stay with me as long as you want.' Rose loved the idea of having a baby in the house.

Ellen tried not to think about the baby which was still not visible in her belly, but one day she felt a pop inside her, like a bubble, like a fish coming up for air.

And then a letter arrived from Wales. Ellen read it and cried out.

'Mammy's in an asylum.'

*

Samuel was angry. They rowed: slammed doors, angry feet stamping on the stairs.

'You're not going back.'

'She's my mother.'

'She has a son as well.'

Ellen tutted in disdain. 'Can you really imagine Bright going home to look after her?'

'We have a life here.'

'You stay then. I'll go on my own.'

She knew he would never countenance that. His dream dashed, he sold the shack at a loss, and with the money he bought two tickets for the *St Lawrence*, bound for the port of Cardiff.

Rose's face was wet when she kissed them goodbye at the dockside. She stayed for a long time after the ship had been tugged out into the Pacific Ocean, waving a silk flowered scarf. Then she turned and walked back up the hill to her house.

Back at home she sat on the balcony in Samuel and Ellen's old room for a while, thinking about the child, the laughter of it, imagining Ellen and Rose bringing her up together. Then she remembered her own dead child. She had mourned her, but not the life she would have brought.

Chapter 28

All at Sea

1888

Something was gone between them, a lightness, a joy.

She slept in the women's berths and he in the men's, so there weren't even those warm wordless nights, the touching of skin, the blending of breath. In the day they sat on deck watching the waves, and spoke little. What was there to speak of? The future was unknown, and the past was lost and best not talked about. They were both adrift. She knew how upset he was to leave San Francisco but she couldn't apologise, for how could she not go to Mammy? She dreamed of the asylum, dark, dripping, echoing with the screams of condemned people. The screams of Mammy.

Day after day, her belly grew slowly, inevitably, like a creeping dread. The berths were cramped and noisy and she couldn't sleep with the sound of the night rantings, the snoring and the farting of strangers. She often crept up on deck and sat hidden away, alone with the sea. The baby kicked heels and fists against her belly as it spun in its own ocean on this ship that ploughed the Atlantic sea towards Cardiff. Aside from shipwreck or miscarriage there was no reversing any of it.

'Belly pork with molasses and beans.' Samuel found her on the deck, bringing her a steaming bowl of stew. She was eating as well as a lady because he had befriended the cook and was squirrelling away portions of the best food for her from the feasts of the captain and his first class passengers.

He sat with her as she ate the stew which was delicious, and they watched the marbled waves awhile, rising and falling. Then he kissed her cheek and went to his berth.

That night, as usual, she got up from her bed. Hannah, the woman in the berth above her, peered over the side of the bunk.

'Where you going now?'

Hannah was used to Ellen's nightly wanderings.

'I ate too much,' said Ellen. 'Beans. My belly feels funny.'

Ellen sat blanket-wrapped on deck. The moonlight brindled the water and a bird sat in the rigging watching her. The feeling in her stomach rose and fell like small breaking waves. She wondered whether the first class passengers were suffering the same effects from the stew.

She started pacing, back and fore across the deck. It helped. A coxswain saw her and ran to tell Samuel. Samuel arrived sleepy on deck, wrapped in a blanket, and saw there was something strange about her, her glittery eyes. He was afraid. 'Come inside. It's cold.'

But she wasn't cold. Her face was shining with moisture.

'You gave me bad pork.'

'This is no pork. You having the baby!'

'What nonsense.' The baby wasn't due for weeks. Not until they were back home with Mammy.

She could not have this baby without Mammy.

Samuel ran, and got Hannah from her bed. When Hannah arrived, she saw a wild woman walking the ship, whispering to herself. Ellen's mouth was dry and salty. The waves inside her were constant now: two synchronised oceans rose and fell. The sweat on her body felt good and cold, her belly between contractions tender, like a half-healed wound. 'Oh blessed Mary,' exclaimed Hannah, and ordered Samuel to get hot water and towels.

'And cold water too, she's dying of thirst.'

Water poured out of her, sloshing on the decks, as Hannah looped an arm round her and took her back to the berths, speaking as though she was a child: 'Hush and be a good girl now. Everything's going to be fine.'

In the berth, Hannah tried to make Ellen lie on her back, but she kept getting up and leaning forward on her arms on the bunk to ease the storm inside her. She wanted to move around but there wasn't room in this low, cramped space.

'Your wife's about as contrary as any I've met,' Hannah told Samuel when he brought the water, giving Ellen a cold soaked towel to suck on. Hush, hush, said Hannah, rubbing Ellen's back with her long bony fingers, so cold and so good.

The pain rose until she was drowning in it, until it was not just inside her but all around her. She felt like an animal, a thrashing captured thing, all language gone. She wanted to go

137

back up on board and launch herself into the sea, but when she tried to stand up her legs buckled under her. She felt something weighing down inside her, something heavy, pushing down, and she started to cry out, oh, oh.

'Come quick!' yelled Hannah and more women came, sleepy from their bunks, to help.

'Get her on the bunk.'

'She won't do it; you have to come down here.'

So the women arranged towels on the floor while Ellen held onto the bars of the bunk for dear life, as though to keep herself from being swept away.

'Oh good god,' said Hannah. 'I can see a head. Look at that black hair.'

'Black hair,' Ellen said from her dream. She wasn't here now; she had drifted to a strange land. The force inside her was getting stronger. Something was stinging but it wasn't hurting her, it was hurting another Ellen who was somewhere else.

And then, just like a great wet fish, the baby schlapped out. Hannah lifted him free of her. He took a gulp and started yelling, at the light, at the noise, at the interruption of his underwater life. After the cord had been cut and the women had bathed him they gave him to her. She sat on the floor, her back against the bunks and held him. He smelt strange, of her, but of inside her; a smell she didn't know. He had a cap of black hair and astonished navy eyes that blinked in the yellow gaslight. She held his fingers, long, like his father's, with nails like jewels. Samuel came and sat beside her and stared and stared and for only the second time since she had known him, she saw tears.

There wasn't much sleep on the ship that night. As Ellen and Samuel gazed at the perfect face of Louis Llewelyn Jordan, the passengers and crew celebrated the birth of Ellen's little pickaninny baby.

For three days she lay on her berth with the baby sucking on her breasts, which were rubbed with lard to ease the soreness, and she wept, a sadness inside her for the whole world; for her dead brother and Samuel's dead brothers and sister, and all the dead babies who had gone before and all who were yet to be born. It was like Louis Llewelyn Jordan had opened a huge chasm of pain inside her. And as she wept the baby watched her, a deep, quiet wisdom in his eyes, and he yawned, the inside of his mouth like a perfect pink shell, and she began to fall in love with the child she had not wanted.

Chapter 29

Louis

1941

Even though he's a grown man, he still loves the story of his birth on the *St Lawrence*.

'Trouble you were, from the minute you arrived,' she jokes now. 'Deciding to make your entrance in the middle of the Atlantic bloody Ocean.'

He stokes the fire for her, puffs up her cushions.

'And I've never been late for anything since.'

'That's true. You're quite the timekeeper.'

He smiles, a special smile that he keeps just for her. His eyes are so deep she can't reach inside this strange, lovely son of hers.

She remembers once smacking his bare backside when she had left him in charge of a pan of sugar and it had burned, because his mind was on something else. Always on something else: his clocks, his camera, his music. She remembers the red handprint on his bottom and Louis looking at her and through her, as though he was remembering every other piece of mistreatment, every flash of anger and spite that had ever come out of her. And he had forgiven her all the same.

She remembers how she held him and cried and said she was sorry, and he had said nothing, his face expressionless. There is something cruel about such forgiveness, she thinks.

As a little boy he liked taking things apart and putting them back together to see how they worked. When Noah brought him a Brownie Box camera he used it to examine the world, taking photographs of tiny things, dust and shadows and fallen leaves, as though he was searching for a secret that might be hidden in the corners.

He rarely played outside, she thinks now. He made a whole world out of the small things inside.

She lost him for a while to the Great War. He was a sapper in Northern France but told her very little about what that was like. After the war he joined the South Irish Horse, a British Army Cavalry regiment in Dublin. She was never quite sure how that happened as he didn't know one end of a horse from the other. He wrote her funny letters about having to go down the tram stairs backwards because of his spurs, and about the one and only time he rode a horse, a sky-high Irish Draught mare, who he was ordered to ride from one side of Dublin to the other. He hung on for dear life, with no idea how to steer this creature, but the mare knew the way and safely delivered him to the designated barracks.

Then he wrote about taking a photograph of a pretty seamstress who was sitting on a sunny bench in Phoenix Park. 'I asked for her address,' he said. 'But only so I could give her a copy of the photograph!'

Ten months later, he brought the pretty woman with the distant eyes, Mary, who was now his wife, home with him to the new house Ellen had bought opposite the graveyard with the proceeds of her sweet shop. And there they had all lived in the years through births and deaths, from that war to this. A life is so long and yet so short, she thinks: so much happens, and so little.

Chapter 30

Asylum

1888

It felt as though she hadn't been away. Everything was familiar: the smell of coal-smoke and horse-piss, the jostle, the heavy sky, the town centre clock gleaming in a rare whisper of sun. They took a cab, and rocked through the town and out into the sodden lanes to the hollow rhythm of the horse's hooves on the wet road. The day became black, leaves flying like red snow. She remembered the salty fogs of San Francisco, and missed them.

Ellen clutched Louis close to her, watching expressions flit over his face as he slept, his fingers curling and uncurling.

'I feel sick,' she said. But it was dread inside her, not bile. Dread, that became heavier as they got closer to the asylum. She remembered the dreams she'd had on the ship, her visions of hell.

And then there it was: an imposing gothic building behind brass gates. The horse pulled up in the courtyard. Samuel stood up to get out but Ellen thrust the baby at him.

'No.'

It was her mother in there: she had to do this. She walked up the path towards the door. Two men raked leaves on the lawn. She hesitated, then pushed it open.

A pink-cheeked nurse in a white apron approached her, smiling.

'I'm here to collect my mother. Mrs Ann Jones.'

'Oh, Ann,' said the woman fondly. 'Of course. Come with me.'

Ellen followed her through dark corridors, the heels of her polished shoes echoing. Click, click, click. Ellen could hear someone screaming from somewhere, but someone was singing too.

The nurse knocked on a door that said 'Medical Superintendent' and they went inside. A man sat behind a desk which had piles of paper files on it, and a telephone with a long curly wire. On the wall was a large clock with a brass cylinder underneath it with paper unfolding from it, marked with pin-pricks like some strange wordless language.

'This is Mrs Ann Jones's daughter,' said the woman.

'Ah, sit down, sit down.' The superintendent waved Ellen to a chair. The nurse hovered near the doorway behind them.

'Is my mother ...'

'Well!' he said. 'Very well.'

He rooted through the files and opened one.

'She was brought in by a neighbour after being found barefoot and incoherent in the middle of the night. But she has been attending church and singing lessons and has been of great help in the laundry. I am happy to discharge her to the care of a relative.'

Ellen nodded.

'She was being held here as a pauper, which means that the bill is covered. But since there is a relative …'

He reached across the desk and handed her an envelope, which she didn't open.

'Nine shillings per week.'

How long has she been in here, Ellen wondered.

'My husband will take care of it.'

'Good. Well …' He nodded and gestured to the nurse. Ellen stood up.

'Thank you, sir.'

He nodded, head down, already absorbed in something else.

Ellen followed the nurse along a maze of dark corridors that smelt unpleasantly of vinegar. She stopped in front of a door, turned to smile at Ellen, and pushed it open.

Inside was a freshly painted room with framed pictures of country scenes on the walls. A group of women – none of whom, Ellen thought, looked mad – sat around a large table in the middle, sewing. There was the whirr of machines and sing-song chatter, a pile of paper dress patterns in the middle of the table. Instead of some vision of hell, it was all quite domestic.

'Ann?'

In the middle of the group was Mammy, who was tacking two pieces of red cotton together. She looked up and saw Ellen.

'Oh, Ellen. How lovely to see you.'

Ellen felt a little fist of fury thump inside her. It was as though she had seen Ellen only last week. What I've given up for you, she thought. How far I've come ...

They followed the nurse's click-click heels back through the corridors, where she retrieved a case from behind a door in the lobby. Ellen took it.

'Thank you.'

And out they went to where Samuel and Louis waited beside the cab.

'This is my son. Louis,' said Ellen. Mammy took him from Samuel's arms without looking at Samuel, held him up to better see his face.

'Oh, look at him. Look at him!'

'Doesn't he look like his daddy?'

'He looks just like himself,' said Mammy, throwing an

invisible cloak around herself, her daughter and her grandson, and blocking Samuel out.

'Just like himself.'

*

The two-up two-down houses in Coke Street were hunched against the rain, small lights from candles and gas-lamps glowing through curtain cracks. Ellen turned the key in the lock of number one and pushed the door open; she heard the scutter of small feet. The house was dark and dank, the floors covered in soot and grime. After they'd lit fires and scrubbed and aired it, it smelled instead of milk and steam, and the walls closed around them.

Ellen and Samuel quarrelled, hissing at one another like cats so as not to wake the baby.

'This asylum bill going to send me bankrupt.'

'I'll ask Bright to pay some of it.'

'Oh and where in the world is Bright? And why should I pay anyway? That woman don't even speak to me.'

'Because she's my mother!'

Every morning, Samuel put on his hat and coat and went out to knock on doors, to stand in queues. The town was growing, bursting out from under its mountains of coal that came down from the valleys. Tunnels and railway lines and buildings were being built and there was plenty of work, building and digging and demolishing and welding. But not for Samuel. Day after day he was politely told he was too young, too old, that the job had already gone. Only once did the employer tell the truth: I don't employ darkies.

At home Ellen was absorbed with her baby in a way she had never thought possible. He held her twisted heart in his small brown fist. She never tired of smelling his hot, sweet hair, gazing at his perfect face, into his quiet eyes. She didn't quite notice Samuel's frustrations at the end of each day when she asked, did you get a job?

'No.'

'You'll get one soon.'

But not soon enough; debt collectors began knocking. So Samuel signed up as a ship's cook again, and left.

Chapter 31

Talking to the Dead

1941

T he bombing continues into the spring, not quite nightly although it feels like it, because even when the bombs don't fall, the family huddles by the fire waiting, waiting for the sirens to sound across the tired city. Every morning brings more awful news: ten people dead in a street near Ellen's old house in Coke Street. Twenty-three people dead in Llanbleddian Gardens and Wyverne Road, families they knew, all gone. On Sunday mornings the bells wake them, discordant and mournful, calling them to church, calling them to pray for it all to end.

Ellen is dressed like a doll and bundled into a bath chair and the family walk to St Peter's for Mass, Mary pushing her, Teresa holding her hand. Louis and Sam walk ahead, chatting, Louis smart in a hat, Sam breaking into a run every few seconds to keep up. The old borrowed chair jolts over the pavement cracks and Ellen's bony fingers grip the arms of the chair against the pain.

Inside the church doorway they bob and make the sign of the cross and pause to light candles for the dead, for the missing, for the living, then settle in a pew at the back so that Ellen's bath chair isn't in anyone's way. The priest chants his Latin laments and they respond, Amen, Amen. Everyone is praying for men to come home, for the war to end, for the Germans to be escorted to hell.

The cries of babies rise to the rafters like balloons and bob around among the sweet incense smoke, the glassy images of God, the stone angels. Sam fidgets, his feet going kick, kick, under the bench, his feet not touching the floor until Mary stops him with an elbow and a glare. Ellen takes communion: the whispering of the priest, a wafer melting on her tongue, a silent prayer.

After Mass they visit Bright in the graveyard opposite their house. Mary lights candles and sits on a bench watching them flicker. There is the breath of spring, shoots pushing up and a piping blackbird. The gravestone reads: *Here lie Bright Jones and Mona Catarina Jones nee Romano. Together forever in the arms of the Lord.* Ellen wonders whether their white bone fingers are reaching out and touching, linked under the earth. When Mona died Bright walked out and didn't stop walking for fifty years. People around the country knew to expect him at the first scent of spring or the shiver of autumn and had jobs ready for him: fences to be mended, potatoes to be dug and walls to be whitewashed in exchange for a hot meal or a new pair of boots.

It was a grand gesture, Ellen thinks. A worthy gift of grief to his wife. All she ever did for Samuel was to just carry on.

But that's what women do. What women have to do. It doesn't mean they love any less.

Silly old bugger: she always expected Bright would die of the cold in some remote barn, or have his throat slit by bandits. Instead he died right outside her front door, looking the wrong way and stepping in front of a tram. Ellen heard a commotion in the street outside and ran out to find him on his back staring up at the sky; the only thing left alive of him was his beard, stirring in the breeze.

The children chase one another, darting like shadows among the trees.

'Stop that,' calls Mary.

'Leave them,' says Louis. 'The dead don't mind. They might even like it.' They might, thinks Ellen. The children's lovely voices, their laughter.

'Remember the plates?' Ellen says. Louis laughs, and Mary says, 'Oh mercy,' and Teresa, hearing them, comes to join in the story, which is one they all tell together, each chipping in a detail, words tumbling over one another in the re-telling of it.

Around Christmas every year Bright arrived bringing strange presents – pine cones, shells, a piece of broken blue crockery. It was all excitement when he came. Ellen prepared a bath while Mary cooked up a feast, cabbage and custard bubbling in the kitchen and a chicken in the oven. After Bright's bath a scissors was produced to make some headway into his hair and beard, the small girl Teresa giggling in his lap. Then there were stories over dinner, so many stories, about lochs in Scotland and village greens in England, and after they would sit in the front room until the fire burned low and everyone was tired. And then Mary would get up to wash the plates. But there was one time when Bright said to her, 'No need, Mary. I licked them all clean and put them back on the dresser for you.'

Mary, staring in horror at all the plates on the dresser.

'I had to get every last one out and wash them again,' she says now. 'Half the night it took me.'

Louis laughs. 'Uncle Bright. One of a kind.'

And the candles flicker, a breath passing through them, as though Bright hears them, smiling down there in the earth.

But there is no gravestone for Ellen to sit beside. He must be so lonely, Ellen thinks. She closes her eyes. She can hear the small voices of birds, the laughter of the children, the chat of Mary and Louis. Come back Samuel, she thinks. Come back and talk to me.

Chapter 32

Rats

1892

There was a rap on the door and Mammy answered it.

'It's the rat-catcher,' she called back into the house. 'Better late than never,' she said to the visitor. 'They're driving me mad. Scritch scratch scritch scratch.' She came back into the house and Ellen wiped her hands on her apron and went to see what was going on. Samuel stood on the doorstep, his hat in his hand, his sea-chest at his feet.

'Oh,' she said, and cupped his face with her palms, touched his hair that had grown springy as heather. She stood back to let him pull his sea-chest into the hall. She laid her head against his chest. Three years, she thought, three years without him. Without this warmth. She took his hand and led him into the front room, and there, sitting on a chair with his feet not touching the ground and dressed in his Sunday best, was Louis.

'This is your father, Louis,' Ellen said.

Louis stared at Samuel with round black eyes. Neither of them spoke, though through Samuel's hand Ellen felt a quickened pulse beat.

'I got you a present,' Samuel said. He opened the sea-chest and took out a box. 'Go on, open it.'

Louis glanced at Ellen and she nodded her approval.

Inside the box was a carved wooden monkey, painted green. 'It's a clock,' said Samuel. 'It's from Malaya, which is in the Far East.' Together father and son silently assembled the clock. The monkey sat on a branch and his tail hanging down was the pendulum. Samuel showed Louis how to wind it up. When the clock was ticking the tail swung and the monkey's eyes moved from side to side.

Tick, tock, tick. Louis watched the monkey for a long time. Mammy was moving round the room putting her ear to the walls. 'Scratch, scratch, scratch, they're driving me mad,' she said.

Louis looked at Samuel.

'We don't have rats,' he whispered. And Samuel gave him a small smile, and for a moment father and son were conspirators.

Ellen had taken over Mammy's sewing jobs. Every day neighbours brought sheets and curtains, frocks and underwear, and Ellen sat by the window with pin-pricked fingers and mended, and mended. The walls had closed tight around her these last three years.

Samuel took them to the fair on Whitchurch common, Louis in the middle of them holding hands. They swung him over muddy puddles: one, two, three, wheee! Louis giggling, kicking his feet. A painted organ played jaunty music and they gasped and awed at the strong woman with her tattooed arms lifting a man above her head, and at the bearded lady in a rose dress fanning herself. Louis rode a flare-nosed horse on the carousel, searching for their faces in the crowd to wave at as the horse spun him round and round. They wandered home as the sun dropped, Louis smelling of sunshine and sugar, and when they got to the house he ran to tell Mammy about the day.

He ran back to find them, in the hallway taking off hats and coats.

'Granny's sleeping.'

Ellen felt something jump inside her: a skipped heartbeat. She ran upstairs and stopped in the doorway. Mammy lay on the bed, her arms crossed over her chest like a saint, staring at the ceiling.

'Oh, Mammy.' Ellen smoothed her hand over Mammy's cold eyes to close them, and then sat on the bed and watched her for a long time. Poor Mammy, who had never been at peace.

At least she had a quiet death, Ellen thought.

Mammy was laid out on the table in the front room. Samuel hitched Louis on his shoulders and they went to the docks to look at the ships. And Ellen, her hands shaking, washed Mammy's cold body with warm soapy water, the smell reminding her of washing her fat giggling baby, and she sang to her like she sang to him, as though Mammy was a child: *Ar Hyd y Nos*. Sleep my child and peace attend thee …

Around her, she felt the demons retreating at Mammy's quietus. Hush now, Mammy. Hush.

Mammy was buried in the Catholic cemetery under the

bowed arms of a yew tree, next to Daddy. Afterwards Samuel took Ellen and Louis to a tearoom for tea and fruit cake where they sat in a shaft of sunlight in the window. The tearoom was warm with the clink of china and chat. There was another family on the next table, a mother, father and a girl with ribbons in her hair, and Ellen thought how very ordinary this all was. Ordinary, and lovely.

On the way home they stopped to look at the animal wall in front of the castle, the life-size painted stone animals on their plinths staring down at passers-by with their glassy orange eyes: a wolf, a lynx, a hyena, two cuddling baboons, a seal, a wide-eyed bear, a regal lioness and two lions bearing coats of arms. Samuel lifted Louis up so he could take a closer look at them and he shrieked and giggled, reaching a hand out, almost daring to touch but then pulling it back.

'Do they bite?'

Ellen laughed.

'They're not real, Louis.'

'Have you ever seen a lion, Daddy?' he asked on the way home, skipping beside them, gripping Samuel's hand.

'I have not,' Samuel said. 'But I've seen a wolf.'

Louis gasped.

'Were you scared?'

'Not so much. The wolf was more scared than me. It had yellow eyes.'

'Yellow eyes!'

'I've seen baboons too. Full of mischief. Steal the clothes off your back if you're not careful …'

Ellen pushed open the door of Coke Street. Samuel's sea-chest stood waiting in the hall, always waiting, always in transit. The house was silent apart from the tick-tock of the green monkey clock, and dark as a burrow. Sunlight rarely reached through the yellowing net curtains into this place. A pile of sheets, clothes and curtains on the sewing table in the window waited to be attended to.

She put a kettle to boil on the stove, poked the coals on the fire to waken them. Louis dragged a chair across the floor and took a globe from the shelf.

'Uncle Noah brought me this.'

'Ah, Uncle Noah. I've not seen him in a long time. I been hoping to cross with him somewhere.'

They lived in a different dimension, these men, she thought. Almost another world. She thought of her own tiny globe, which had shrunk in the last three years and which could now be crossed in a morning.

As she made tea, Louis and Samuel sat at the table with their heads bent over the globe, and Samuel traced his finger around it to show Louis where he was going next. Across the blue Atlantic sea, around Cape Horn, and up around South America to San Francisco.

'This is San Francisco,' he said. 'Your mother and I lived there for a few years.'

It was as though he was talking about someone else.

Later, when Louis was in bed, they sat in the crackling silence, Samuel reading, Ellen sewing.

She put the sewing down and watched him for a long time, wondering whether there was a way of getting to where they had been, or even somewhere new. Somewhere away from here, this small patch of warmth with the cold and dark closing in around them, where she would soon be alone.

'Can we come with you?' she asked.

He put his book down.

'Louis is too small.'

She thought of Rusty, dead at her feet, and the dying woman in her berth, and the sky-high walls of marbled water crashing down on the deck. She nodded.

'Stay then.' Let us be a family she thought, with fairground visits and quarrels and a warm bed at night.

'And do what? Beg in the streets?'

Three days later Samuel boarded a ship to San Francisco, leaving Ellen and Louis alone. They had no idea when they would see him again.

Chapter 33

News

1892

M^{y dear Ellen}, he wrote.

I am in San Francisco, and wishing you were beside me, and imagining that you are. It has lost something of its charm without you here.

But I have news. I met Rose, and quite by accident. I went to her boarding house but she has sold it and it is in need of some care, and quite seedy, so I took a room near Montgomery Street, where I quite by chance met her in the street. She is now the proprietor of a Fine Dining Establishment and I joined her for dinner there. It is opulent and very beautiful and the food is French-inspired. She has made a great success of it and we passed a pleasant evening. She asked after you and Louis and hopes that one day you will make the journey to see her again.

Tomorrow I set sail on the cargo ship Barraccus. *We are headed for Hamburg with a cargo of wheat, and from where I shall write to you again.*

I hope you think of me.

Your loving husband, Samuel.

It didn't do, she had decided, to have regrets, because you couldn't go back and change things, and the thinking would drive you mad. But she missed Rose, and she missed San Francisco, and she wondered what their lives might have been if they'd stayed, as Samuel had wanted.

Chapter 34

Guests

1892

The chickens knew what was coming and scattered, but not fast enough and she grabbed one and twisted its neck, feeling the small bones snapping under her fingers. Its wings flapped as she carried it inside, as though in death it could finally fly. 'I'm sorry,' she told it. But guests were coming. She slit its neck and drained the bird of its warm metal-scented blood, dunked it in warm water and sat down to pluck it.

Guests were coming. This dark little house, which held her like a rock holds a fossil, was going to be split open with music and laughter. Noah had taken Louis to meet Bright and Mona from their ship and bring them home. She kept the small back room just for Noah, as he was working for the Dublin General Steamship Company on the carrier ships to Dublin and Liverpool, so he was often in Cardiff. The two women across the road gossiped: 'She's living with a darkie who's not even her husband. It's a bloody scandal!' Silly women, she thought, remembering Rose, the midnight men coming out of her room with clothes askew. They wouldn't know a scandal if it bit them on the behind.

It upset her when they dragged their children away from Louis, but she wasn't going to think about that now.

The chicken was naked as a newborn. She felt her way into its still-warm belly and scooped out its intestines. She wondered what Samuel was doing now: was he sleeping, or watching the sea, or was he preparing food like her, pulling apart something that had been alive. She closed her eyes for a moment, tried to feel the creak and roll of the ship underneath her. She imagined all the seas she hadn't yet travelled: the Mediterranean, the Indian Ocean, the South China Sea, the Arctic, the Southern Ocean. And all the seas within seas: the Sea of Marmara, the Black Sea, the Arabian, the Red, the Coral. The places she had wanted to travel until … Until.

She put the chicken in a pan to boil. Then she kneaded dough with her knuckles and put it in the oven to fatten. She scrubbed the bedsheets in the stone sink and hung them out across the yard where they flew, happy as flags. She poked a feather duster into corners, swept floors, shook out curtains. She emptied the coin jar and ran down the street to buy a flagon of home-brewed ale from Mr Lewis, and then, on a whim, bought a string of bright string-wrapped pink onions from a passing Onion Johnny and hung them in the kitchen. Then she sat in the window and waited.

She heard the horse's hooves slowing on the road outside and ran out to greet them. Louis was sat on Bright's lap, arms locked around his neck. Bright set him on the ground and he and Noah lifted Bright's sea-chest from the trap. Then Bright extended an arm out and helped Mona down. She moved stiffly, as though she had grown old.

Ellen rushed to hug Bright and then Mona. She felt Mona's thinness under her coat.

'I'm so happy,' said Ellen.

'I am too,' said Mona. 'But if you don't mind, I'm tired from the journey, if I could lie down for an hour?'

Her eyes were moist, and there were drops of sweat on her face, like rain on glass. Her pretty lips were stone-dry and cracked. Ellen took her upstairs, to the bed she had prepared, helped her off with her coat and lit a candle which threw shadows on her gaunt face.

'I'm sorry,' Mona said. 'We have fun tomorrow.'

That night there was no laughter and no music. Ellen, Bright and Noah sat quiet under the gaslight, Ellen shushing Louis so Mona wasn't disturbed, and upstairs Mona coughed, and coughed.

'She caught a bad cold on the ship,' said Bright, pulling on his pipe and watching the flames flutter on the coals.

Noah had brought Louis a wooden yacht with white sails and the next day they went to the river to sail it. Noah crouched on the shore with Louis watching the yacht drifting among the ducks, Louis giggling because the ducks were bigger than the boat. Bright and Mona sat on a bench. Ellen thought of the time they were all in San Francisco together and missed Samuel with a sudden awful ache, but this wasn't the same as San Francisco, those carefree days. Everyone was different and Mona coughed into a handkerchief and the joy was gone from her.

That evening the doctor was called.

Chapter 35

Mice

1892

My dear husband,

I am sorry to tell you that I have sad news. Mona has died. She and Bright came to visit not long after you left. Bright was bereft to have missed Mammy's funeral and we visited her grave. Mona was not looking well; she was thin and pale, and that lovely light in her eyes was dulled. They stayed awhile and she did not get any better so we called in the doctor, who told us what I had feared, that she had consumption. He suggested a stay in the sanatorium – he said it was best that she didn't stay in our home because of the risk of passing it on to Louis. And indeed, in the garden of the sanatorium I saw sick children, which is one of the saddest things I have ever seen, and I am happy to be able to tell you that Louis remains healthy in body and mind.

We were told that Mona would get better with the diet and rest she would be given in the sanatorium but once there her health deteriorated very quickly until she could not catch her breath at all. She had been there merely a few weeks before she passed away.

Bright has lost his mind over this. He believes she caught the disease on the ships, and that it is his fault. He said he was going to walk, and keep on walking. He packed a small bag and left, and I have not heard from him since. I am worried, but also sure that he will return when he is ready.

Thank you for the news of Rose. I miss her as though she were my own sister.

And I miss you too, and pray that God will keep you safe until you return to me.

I am, as always, your loving wife

Ellen.

The house was quiet again, and cold. In the night she held Louis close to her for warmth and listened to the night-time city, the trains calling eerily into the dark.

Samuel sent postcards, from the Americas, from the grand cities of Europe, from Constantinople, India, China. The cards told of storms and suicides, pirates and stowaways, mutinies and wrecks. In one card he told her they were wrecked off the coast of Australia. He was safe, as were all the passengers and crew, and while he awaited another ship, he was staying in an Aboriginal village.

Ellen and Louis read the cards, poured over the pictures of domed cities and arid deserts and people who spoke languages they didn't understand and lived in ways they could not know. They traced Samuel's journeys with their fingers across Noah's small globe, and imagined, and imagined.

Once a month Ellen crossed the moor to the docks to collect her small allowance from the Shipping Office. At home she sat in the window looking out onto the grey street, watching the neighbours coming and going, the women standing tiptoe on stools washing train-yard grime from their windows, the boys kicking stuffed stockings around the gutters, and she waited for customers to call. But a new garment factory had opened up down the road, employing women to work long hours for a pittance, and they could do the jobs Ellen used to do at less cost.

Ellen came into the kitchen to see Louis kneeling on the floor pouring water onto a mountain of spilled sugar. She grabbed his arm and yanked him to his feet.

'What are you doing?'

He looked at her, woken from a world he had been lost in, and then she saw he had made an island out of sugar, with animals that she could not quite identify on it.

And that's how it started. Ellen whisked a bowl of egg whites and icing sugar, and the two of them sat at the table sculpting little sugar mice with wool tails. When the mice had set, they went out onto the street to sell them.

'their heart grew cold

they let their wings down'

Sappho

Chapter 36

Sweet

1899

Louis called into the house. 'Mammy, there's someone at the door.'

Ellen came into the hallway, brushing flour off her hands onto her apron.

'Oh Louis, you silly boy, this is your father.'

Louis eyed his father suspiciously before disappearing into the house. 'Oh, come in,' said Ellen, taking Samuel's hands and pulling him inside. He is thin, she thought, his skin dry with a grey pallor. He had been away a long time, and his journeys had been hard.

After he had bathed he gave Louis a boomerang he had brought from Australia and Louis went out to the moorland to play with it. Ellen brought him tea and they sat together at the table, two strangers.

'I have something for you.'

From his pocket he took out a small blue bottle. Inside it was a tiny wooden ship.

'I made it.'

'You made this?'

Beyond cooking, making things was never Samuel's passion. He preferred to use his mind. But he remembered how much she had loved the little ships in bottles.

'Look at the smoke,' he said. The ship had a small curl of smoke coming from the chimney. A curl of Samuel's own hair, which was greying at the temples.

She gripped the bottle in her palm.

'I will treasure this forever.'

Then: 'I have a surprise for you, too.'

Ellen took Samuel down the road to a small shop on the corner and unlocked the door with a large brass key. Inside, she pulled up the blind. Light came in streams through the window illuminating jars of bright things. Sweets. Boiled sweets, mint cake, peanut brittle, jelly beans, wine gums, fudge, marzipan, brandy balls, clove rocks, pear drops, coconut ice, bonbons, chocolate limes, violet lozenges, lime fruit, twists of barley sugar.

He looked around him. Dust danced in slats of sunshine.

'This is yours?'

She nodded, watching his face carefully: was he pleased? From under the counter she brought a tray of homemade toffee, smashed it with a hammer, and handed him a piece.

'How you afford it?'

'I saved every penny you sent me. And a benefactor lent me some money.'

Samuel rolled the piece of toffee between his fingers.

'A benefactor?'

'He is called Mr Laird.'

She saw a shadow of something pass over his face.

'And sugar is cheap,' she said.

'I know it.'

She wished she hadn't said that. She stepped towards him and put her arms around him. Through his shirt she could smell his skin, that scent she thought she could never forget, but when he was gone from her she could never quite bring it to mind. She could hear him breathing.

He is tired, she thought.

In the night, when he touched her, it felt like her body had turned to rain.

'I've missed you,' she whispered into the darkness. 'I've so missed you.'

He was silent for a long time and then he said, 'The next ship I am taking is to Cape Town.'

'Cape Town? Africa?'

'Africa.'

Ellen had told Louis that one day they would go to all the places on Noah's globe and see things even stranger than the ones they had imagined.

But Louis was only ten.

'Louis has to go to school.'

'He'll learn more on the ship than he ever will in school.' Samuel was speaking into her hair. She could feel his warm breath. 'He is growing without me.'

'It's dangerous.'

'There's danger whether you're on the sea or the land.'

'I have a business to run.' The shop was doing well. Children saved their pennies to fill their mouths with sticky delights; women came to buy gifts; men came to buy something sweet to atone for misdemeanours.

'I had a business once.'

He will never let me forget that shack in the hills, she thought.

'Just let's enjoy this time together,' she said.

'So you don't want to come.'

'What d'you mean I don't want to? D'you think I like being left here on my own? D'you think I don't get lonely?'

'I get lonely, too.'

She laughed. 'Even with women like Ernestina in the world?'

He moved away from her. She could feel him watching her in the dark.

'Ernestina?'

'I'm sure there are plenty more.'

She didn't know why she was saying these things. She hadn't known she felt like this, but a bitter thing was rising in her, like her anger at Bright when he had left her for the sea all those years ago.

'A girl in every port. Isn't that what they say?'

He turned away from her onto his back. She could see his profile against the grey dark of the room.

'That's what they say,' he said.

And the secret velvety warmth of the bedroom melted away and the town crept back in through the gaps in the window panes, with all its spite and smoke stench.

Chapter 37

Ugly

1899

S amuel asked lots of questions about Mr Laird.

'How did you meet him?'

'Louis and I were selling sweets from a street-stall and he stopped by to talk.'

'What does he do?'

'He owns a factory.'

'What is his wife like?'

'He is a widower.'

When the dinner invitation arrived, she dismissed it.

'I'll say we're busy.'

'Why?' asked Samuel. 'You don't want him to meet me?'

And so it was on a warm summer evening that Mr and Mrs Jordan dressed in their best clothes and took a cab across town to a large house overlooking a lake. They were shown into a sumptuous drawing room where Mr Laird, an oversized man with a veiny face and eyes, introduced them to the rest of the guests.

'This is Mrs Ellen Jordan, the proprietor of a confectionary shop, and her husband Samuel.' The guests smiled and nodded and stared and then turned their backs, made surprised faces at one another, and resumed their conversations.

Oh god, thought Ellen. We shouldn't have come.

A servant brought them sherry in little cut-glass tumblers. The other guests kept glancing at them curiously but didn't come near, and Ellen stayed close to Samuel, wishing she could spit the sherry out. Might as well drink vinegar, she thought. Samuel drank his in one go.

Mr Laird's voice carried over everything. When he spoke he kept his voice raised, so that everyone in the vicinity could hear his important conversation. When Ellen had first met him she had thought him charming, but now, here, showing off in his drawing room, she knew that Samuel found him vulgar. Why did we come? she wondered.

She pointed out all of Mr Laird's lovely things to Samuel, just for something to say, so they didn't stand there silent. Look at the lovely gold mirror. Look at the patterns on that rug. Look at …

Samuel walked over to a shelf and picked something up.

'What is this,' he asked, his voice rising above the party babble.

'Put it down,' said Ellen, quietly, still smiling. But he didn't put it down. The guests stopped mid-conversation.

The thing Samuel was holding was a ceramic penny jar in the shape of the head of a black man, eyes bulging and showing the whites, and his mouth, where the pennies were placed, was wide and red with an ugly drooping lower lip. The base of the jar was two hands, outstretched. Begging.

'Put it down,' hissed Ellen again. Everyone was staring.

'This ugly thing. Is this how you see me?'

Mr Laird smiled at his guests as someone might smile if a child was misbehaving.

'Is this how you see all of us, who have broken our backs to build your so-called great nation? To stuff your fatty-fat faces with cheap sugar?'

There was a gasp from the guests. Hands flew over mouths.

'Stop it!' whispered Ellen.

Mr Laird stepped out from the crowd of open-mouthed, thrilled guests.

'It's just an ornament, Sammy. It means nothing.'

'Nothing? It means nothing? No. This is how you see people like me. And because of that no one will give me a job. I have seen my son three times in nine years. When I come home he doesn't recognise me. Is that nothing? I work my fingers to the bone but still you see me like this, indolent and stupid and beg-begging for every penny. Is that nothing?'

For a moment Ellen thought he would break the thing, but he put it back on its plinth, gently, where it grinned its ugly, stupid grimace at the watching crowd.

'Sammy, please …' said Mr Laird.

'My name is Samuel.' Spoken slowly, with deliberation. And he turned and walked out. And Ellen, knowing they had provided the entertainment for the evening, that the dinner party would be remembered as the best for many years because of them, mumbled, 'I'm sorry,' and ran after him.

She found him leaning on a rail and staring at the lap-lap of the lake.

'How could you do that?'

He turned to look at her. His face was lost in sorrow.

'Come with me,' he said. 'Come with me on the *Sunningdale*.'

'I have a child to look after.'

'Louis, too, of course,' he said.

'The boy needs to go to school. The boy needs a structured life.'

He looked at her then.

'What has become of you? Where is my wild girl?'

'I'm not a girl, I'm a woman. I have responsibilities. A business to run.'

'We don't belong here,' he said. 'We're strangers.'

'No, Samuel Jordan, you're the stranger, behaving like that. He welcomed you into his home ...'

'I'm the stranger?'

'Yes.'

There was a long pause. And then Samuel turned and walked away.

By the time she got home he had already left, his sea-chest gone from the hall. Good riddance, she thought. The shame of it. Every time she thought about it little hot waves shot through her veins. I will never forgive him for this.

There was a knock at the door. He has come to say sorry, she thought. If he is sorry enough I will forgive him. She opened the door and folded her arms across her chest.

But it wasn't Samuel come to say sorry. It was Noah, come to find him.

Chapter 38

Noah

1941

Ellen dozes in her chair by the window to the sound of Teresa's pencil scratching in her schoolbook and the coals spitting in the fire. When she wakes Noah is sitting opposite her.

'Shall I get Mary to make a cup of tea?' he asks, and she nods, not because she wants tea but because she knows he wants to do something. She watches him walk stiffly to the door on his bandy sea-legs.

Noah has always been here, she thinks.

His face is salt-sketched, and his eyes are becoming milky. He always looks as though he is watching something just out of reach, something no one else can see.

Teresa on the floor by the fire, groans at her schoolbook.

'I hate arithmetic,' she says. 'Why do we have to learn it?'

'How would you know how much change the bus driver has to give you without arithmetic?' asks Noah, coming back in.

'When I grow up,' says Teresa, 'I won't go on buses. I'll have a motor car.'

'You need to buy that motor car.'

Teresa groans again.

'Granny, were you good at sums?'

'Course she was,' says Noah. 'How d'you think she ran her sweet shop without arithmetic? It's important.'

Ellen half-listens. She is forgetting so much, but not the treasures that she holds inside of her. The rise of a wave, the breath of an iceberg, the scent of a man's skin. Those are the things that are important, she thinks.

'You have to go to sea,' she says. Teresa sits up, happy to leave her schoolwork.

'What if I don't meet a sailor?'

'You don't need a sailor. Just go and do it. Go out and see that beautiful world.'

She remembers: a flock of albatross diving, a moon without a face, gaslight on a man's skin.

'You can do anything you want.'

But *she* didn't. She could have gone with Samuel when he asked her to. And even after that, when Louis was grown she could have gone, boarded a ship, sailed away. Why didn't she?

But she knows why. It was because Samuel would always have been there, in the shadows of the galley, a bird in the rigging, a step ahead of her on the deck. He would have been there, but just out of her reach.

Teresa smiles at the idea that she could do anything. And Ellen wants that for her. Don't be afraid, she thinks.

'You might even see angels that aren't made of stone,' says Ellen.

Noah laughs.

'Me and Samuel never saw us no angels. Samuel thinks it was Old Joe putting nonsense in your head.'

'I know what I saw.'

What treasures does he hold in his head, she wonders. She has known him nearly all her life. He never forgets a birthday and knows just what will make the perfect present – a camera for Louis, an atlas for Teresa, a train set for Sam, a piece of silk for Ellen, all the way from China.

He knows this family better than they know him.

He never married. Has there ever been a woman? she wonders. Did he ever go to those houses in the ports where the seamen go? She hopes so, but she can't imagine it. Neither he nor Samuel ever spoke those filthy words that the other seamen used. But if ever a man deserved warmth, it was Noah. She asked him once and he told her there was someone, but that it could never be. She sensed he didn't want to tell her more, so she didn't pry.

After she bought this house she kept a room here for him for whenever he came ashore. This house, opposite the graveyard, with no neighbours opposite, where only the dead watched them.

Not that she cared what anyone thought. She loved Noah like a brother, and they could think what they bloody well wanted.

Chapter 39

Lost

1899

It was two days after Samuel left that Louis didn't come in for his tea. She walked round the streets calling him, panic rising. And then, in a back alley, she saw him.

Her son, her Louis Llewelyn, her dreamy boy who photographed shadows, who collected maps, who took apart clocks to see how they worked, was in the middle of a group of boys who were punching him, making monkey noises, telling him to go back to the jungle. His dreamy smile was gone but still he didn't cry. He looked stunned, as though he had woken and found himself somewhere unfamiliar.

Ellen felt her heart crack in two.

She pulled the boys off by their collars, slapped the ringleader hard around the face. She wished she was Rose, who would have had something clever to say. But instead she said, 'You had all better get yourselves to church to think hard on your wickedness. And if I ever see this again you won't even be in a fit state to go crying to your mothers.'

At home she washed Louis' cuts with salt water.

I called him a stranger, she thought.

What have I done?

They took the train to Barry. It was slow, inexorably slow, stopping at every station, happy chatty people getting on and off. Hurry, she thought. Hurry. Louis watched her face, knowing something was wrong but not daring to ask.

At last, the train arrived at Barry and they ran down the windy hill to the port. Gripping Louis' hand tight she searched the smoky sweat-scented seamen's bars searching for Samuel. Men jeered and laughed at her, shouting crude words, pretending they thought she was a prostitute. But a barman took pity on her, asking what she was looking for.

'My husband,' she said. 'He is due to sail on the *Sunningdale*.'

'The *Sunningdale* has sailed.'

Sailed and taken her husband. All she had left of him was the curl of his hair on the funnel of the ship in the blue bottle.

*

My dear husband, she wrote.

I hardly know what to say to you. There seems a huge rift between us, wider than the oceans you travel.

I want to tell you I know I was wrong. I allowed embarrassment to cloud my judgement. I have informed Mr Laird that I will pay every penny back that I owe him, and I will borrow no more.

I hope you find some peace as you travel down the coast of

Africa. I will be with you in spirit, and one day I will come with you and see Africa for myself.

There is so much more I want to say to you but I cannot find the words.

Until we meet again

Your loving wife

Ellen.

She waited and waited for his letter. In the night she dreamed of the ugly thing; it taunted her. What happened to the wild girl who was me, she wondered; the girl who stood up to Mrs Watkins. Where did she go?

She wrote another letter. This time, it was like a plea. Forgive me, she thought as she wrote it: forgive me.

My darling husband, this life has been hard on us. I wanted to tell you that I will come with you again, when Louis is old enough. I would like to visit India, and Australia, and Africa, and all the other places you have described to me. I think of our time on the ships and it seems now like a dream, that I could have done that with you. We had such happy times together. And we will do again. Your loving wife Ellen.

At night she closed her eyes and tried to fly to join him, like she did when she was a child, flying over the sparkling sea to be with Bright. But now, she couldn't fly. Her mind was too heavy.

At last, a letter arrived, posted in Cape Town.

She opened it.

But it wasn't from him.

*

Noah brought the death certificate some months later. She read it and read it as though there might be a clue hidden in the words somewhere. But there was nothing. There was the name of the ship, the *Sunningdale*, and the date of his death, the 19th of September. There was the place of death – 13° 22′ N, 26° 28′ W, which when she looked on a map was not a place at all, but a lonely expanse of blue off Cape Verde.

Then under 'Cause of Death' was written, in careful handwriting: 'Through excessive drinking whilst in the port of Barry, not eating any food became that weak till he died.'

Noah didn't understand it.

'He lost his mind,' he said.

He'd been raving, Noah said. 'He said he had nothing left to live for. He said that always, his whole life, he would be a stranger. What did he mean?' wondered Noah. But Ellen knew.

And then, in Noah's view the only lucid thing he had said, he made Noah promise to look after Ellen, to make sure no harm came to her.

He thought of me even when he was dying, she thought.

I didn't deserve that.

She took Louis to the seaside and sat on the sea-wall and watched the suck of the tide while Louis searched for treasure among the stones. He ran towards her, triumphant, bright-faced and salty-haired, clutching something in his hand; a creature, curled in a perfect spiral inside its stone home.

'Look! I found a fossil!'

She took it from him and smiled, ran her fingers over its smooth salt-washed surface.

'How old is it?' he asked.

'I don't know. Old.'

'A million years?'

'Maybe.'

'A billion?'

'Could be.'

They both looked at it, this small thing that had once been alive, peaceful in its quietude. Then Louis stuffed it in his pocket and ran off to find more.

She hadn't yet told him that his father was dead.

A few years later, he asked her: 'Why did Dad do that?'

'Sometimes, when a terrible thing is done, there is a wound so great it travels through the generations. A scar that cannot heal. Do you know what I mean?'

And Louis put his hand on his heart and nodded. 'I feel it.'

But now, as he squatted on the rocks peering into dark pools of water, he didn't yet realise he had a scar.

A ship idled on the horizon. The sea was quiet and brown, not blue like the painted sea on the globe. She breathed with it and felt it breathe back with her.

'Keep my husband safe,' she whispered, and the sea shivered with the weight of all the secrets it had to keep. Ellen remembered what Samuel had told her about the garden of bones of the African slaves on the ocean bed, and she thought, he has joined them. All he wanted was to be home, and I denied him that.

But he is home now.

Chapter 40

Blue

1941

Ellen dreams a lot, thinks a lot, sitting in the window in an armchair. There's nothing else to do.

In the cemetery over the road a man is bent, digging a grave. When she slips into sleep she too bends, plunges her fingers into the earth. She is back at Coke Street digging for potatoes. But under the earth she finds Samuel's brothers and sister, anguished, scratching in the dark dust, trying to crawl out into the light.

She wakes with a cry at their distress. In the graveyard the man still digs among graves hunched as monks, and dreaming stone-eyed angels. There are daffodils, bright against the granite and marble.

Trams rattle past, a woman holding hands with a small child, a cat leaping over the wall and disappearing to search for mice among the tombstones. And then she sees a girl she recognises. Blonde tangled hair, dirty white socks. She raps on the window and the girl stops, looks. Ellen indicates with her fingers: come here. The girl looks up and down the street, unsure, and then approaches the front door.

Ellen waits. She doesn't know what she will do, or say.

She imagines what Rose might say, imagines the girl stunned and cowed by her great mind. But I don't have a great mind, she thinks. If I had then everything, everything would have been different.

She hears the front door click open, then quietly shut, and then the girl is there, in the doorway.

'Come in,' says Ellen.

The girl moves into the room, stands by the bed. The skin below her eyes looks blue and bruised, as though she has been crying, or hasn't slept.

'You're a friend of Teresa's, aren't you,' says Ellen. The girl's eyes widen a bit, but she nods.

'What's your name?'

'Rosalind.'

'What a pretty name.'

She tries to remember. There was another Rosalind. She remembers her feet next to Rosalind's feet. Clear water. She remembers fish.

She doesn't remember what colour the fish were.

'Rosalind what?'

'Davies.'

Ah. Ellen knows the family. They have two boys away

fighting and one of them is missing. Ellen knows what that's like. She remembers waiting for news of Louis from France. The girl chews at a nail. The man in the graveyard is still digging, the mound of earth beside him growing higher.

She tries to remember the other Rosalind. She wonders what has happened to her, what sort of life she had.

She was kind to me, she remembers.

And then Ellen knows what to do.

'Feel under the mattress. There's something there.'

Now the girl looks suspicious.

'Go on.'

Rosalind puts her hand under the mattress and rummages, glances at Ellen, tries again. She pulls out a large leather purse. She hands it to Ellen who clicks it open and looks inside, at the shiny round coins.

Footsteps in the hall and Teresa bursts in, her face full of laughter, roses in her cheeks.

'Granny ...' She stops, stares at Rosalind.

Ellen snaps the purse shut again.

'This war is tiring everybody out. You are going on a family day out to the seaside, and Rosalind is coming too.'

And Rosalind turns and smiles at Teresa, a real smile with no spite hidden behind it.

*

The pain in Ellen's hip, once icy, is hot now, feverish, little rivers of lava. She can hear the family getting ready, Mary fussing about coats and hats.

'Thank you Granny,' says Teresa, kissing her cheek. 'We'll tell you all about it later.'

But Ellen already knows all about it. The family – her family – Louis, Mary, Teresa, Sam, Noah and Reggie the dog, will knock on the Davies's front door to call for Rosalind. And together they will walk through the town to the station, stopping briefly to stare at the ruins of the latest bombing. Teresa and Rosalind will be shy together at first but will start talking, carefully at first, then in rushed, giggling sentences. By the time they reach the railway station they will be linking arms. They will get on the train to Penarth. Some of the passengers will look at them curiously, this family of many colours.

They will stroll through the ornamental gardens down to the promenade where they will cheer the destroyers leaving the port under black smoke, channel water churning before them. Noah will show them where a dead German soldier was found, face down in the shingle, and will help Sam search for shrapnel among the stones while Mary and Louis sit on a bench, their shoulders touching, watching the soft horizon, listening to the lap-lap of the quiet tide and throwing a ball for Reggie, who will lose it among the shallow rock pools. Teresa and Rosalind will search for rainbow-coloured shells, and discover that they love the same books and hate the same teacher. Then they will throw pebbles into the waves and imagine sailing away on a ship. 'We can do it,' Teresa will tell her. 'We can do anything we want.'

Everyone will gather round to admire a thrashing fish a boy has caught.

And then they will go into the steamy Rabaiotti's for Mary's favourite frothy coffee, and hot chocolate and a plate piled high with cakes, because the cafes aren't rationed like everywhere else.

Later that night, or another night, back in the bomb shelters Rosalind will remember her lovely day with Teresa's family; will remember Noah's stories and Louis' silly jokes and Sam's excitement over his shrapnel treasures, and sitting on the seawall with Teresa swinging their legs and laughing at everything and nothing. And she will remember that this family, for just one day, made her forget the terrible ache of her missing brother.

And the next time the other girls start to make jokes about the tar brush, she'll say 'Leave it out,' and turn away.

Ellen closes her eyes and watches them all from high above, tiny figures in a toy town, but even at this height she can hear their laughter and she knows they will survive this war and will live many years after. Then she's flying above the world, and it's a beautiful thing from so high, the sea veined with sea wash from the tiny ships crossing the planet.

She flies and sea-spray blows through her. She is a wandering kite carried by the wind, flying until there's nothing but blue, to a place where someone lies quiet, waiting for her. Maybe we'll be angels, she thinks; together, riding the world's rigging.

THE END

Acknowledgements

I'd like to extend a huge thank you to the Hay Festival project Writers at Work, funded by Arts Council of Wales, supported by Literature Wales and led by the brilliant Tiffany Murray. The scheme was life-changing and I'm not sure I'd have written a word of this book without it. And to all the writers I met on this programme, you are too many to mention but you know who you are: thank you for your generosity in sharing your work, and in reading mine.

To Alys Conran, who tutored me on a novel-writing course at Tŷ Newydd, thank you for your support, enthusiasm and magnanimity.

To Rhian Elizabeth, Clare Potter, Rebecca Parfitt, Louise Walsh and Fizzy Oppe, thank you for the laughter, wine, encouragement and friendship: I hope I give as much to you as you do to me.

To my partner Poli Cárdenas: thank you for embracing the chaos and keeping everything afloat.

And a special thanks to my wonderful editor, Rebecca F. John, for the tireless and meticulous care you took of me and my book.

When *Salt* was accepted for publication I tried to track down my old English teacher from Llanedeyrn High School to tell her. Many years ago she recognised a writer in me, and did her best to nurture me, but in those days I was adrift. Sadly I was too late as she had passed away some years previously, but I'd like to think that somehow she knows.

A great teacher stays with us always. Miss Calford, thank you.